Sabrina Fludde

Sabrina Fludde

Pauline Fisk

BLOOMSBURY

First published in Great Britain in 2001 by Bloomsbury Publishing Plc
38 Soho Square, London, W1D 3HB

Copyright © Pauline Fisk 2001

The moral right of the author has been asserted
A CIP catalogue record of this book is available from the British Library

ISBN 0 7475 5523 0

Printed in Great Britain by Clays Ltd, St Ives plc

1 3 5 7 9 10 8 6 4 2

For David

'The ancients had river gods; we too have them in our minds and feel their qualities. For rivers are things of life and personality, of soul and character.'

A.G. Bradley, *The Book of the Severn*
(Methuen, 1920)

Part One
River Mist

A body on the water

When the day began the body was there. The night mist parted and it floated slowly on the silent river like a tree snapped at the root. Its hair spread across the water like a halo of little branches. Its face was deathly white. Its eyes stared like knots of wood, shiny and unseeing as a town approached.

The flourishing market town of Pengwern; when it was a city and a fortress, its watchmen would have noticed anything that came rolling downriver from the Welsh mountains. But its modern skyline looked down upon the body without seeing it. Even when the early morning mist began to melt, it made no difference.

The body floated towards the town and nobody saw a thing. It floated past water meadows where early morning walkers exercised their dogs. Past the water tower which marked the approach to the town. Past steep-gardened houses where curtains were drawn back for the new day, toasters popping, kettles boiling, radios and television sets blaring out the morning news. But nobody paused to look down from their windows and see anything unusual in the river.

Even the wildfowl on the water failed to see anything amiss – moorhens dabbling in the shallows as if the body weren't there, and swans floating past, stately and unperturbed. A heron swooped low, casting a ghostly shadow over the body, and a white gull landed on its shoulder, hitching a ride, its eyes peeled for fish.

But as if it didn't know or care what happened to it, the body floated on, carried by the river until the town rose overhead. It stood like an island in a horseshoe loop in the river – a jumble of towers and spires, castle walls and new shopping malls, medieval mansions, and train and bus stations. The river carried the body past them all – and nobody saw anything! Not on the main road, packed full of morning traffic. Not on the Welsh Bridge, where cars inched nose to bumper into town.

Even when the body passed beneath the bridge and swept on to the Quarry Park, nobody noticed anything. Here, cyclists pedalled beneath avenues of trees and mothers pushed babies. Leaves fell like snowflakes into the river, and everybody turned to watch. But no one saw a body floating through the leaves.

It was as if the body weren't there, floating on its way without caring what happened or knowing where it was. It floated past a school with girls out on the hockey pitch, but never waved to them for help. Floated past a boat club, but never called to its rowers on the water. Floated past a row of tennis courts, but never tried to attract its players as it flowed on round the town.

Finally the castle appeared, viewed from the English Bridge on the east side of Pengwern. By now the morning rush hour was easing off and there were fewer people about to see a body drifting along. But a policeman leant over the bridge, and he didn't notice anything. And a lone cyclist took the river path on the far side of the bridge, and he never once glanced at the body which was starting down the straight stretch to the town's last bridge.

The old, iron-girdered railway bridge.

Here, caught beneath the shadows of the castle, the river began to change. A thin wind blew up it, scuffing the water into rows of sharp waves which ran between the high fence of a football pitch and a treeless path beneath the old town walls. The body started down this gloomy stretch of water, and the waves broke over it, knocking it about.

No longer did it float serenely, like a dead queen on her funeral journey. It shook like a rag doll, bobbed like a plastic bottle, took in water like a sinking ship. It went under water and came up again. Went down again – *and started struggling at long last.*

The body wasn't dead, after all. *It was alive.* Its eyes blinked out water, and its shoulders hunched against the waves. Its hands rose in a plea for help, and its head turned, revealing a face.

It was a child's face. *A little girl's.*

She let out a cry, as thin as the wind. But nobody heard. The paths were deserted on either side of the river, with no more cyclists in sight. There was not a figure on the castle walls, and even the policeman had gone from the English Bridge. Only the pigeons looked down from the fast-approaching railway bridge. But whether they saw the girl, it was impossible to tell.

She bobbed towards them, drawing closer all the time, swept along on a white-water ride. Just as the darkness of the bridge was about to fall on her, a woman with a push-chair suddenly emerged from the tunnel which ran under the bridge. The girl saw her and fluttered her hands, trying to attract attention. But the woman didn't see her. She just hurried on. Even the child in her push-chair didn't see anything.

It was as if the girl weren't there, out in the middle of the river. A race walker emerged from the tunnel, too, shoulders tight, buttocks swinging. The girl tried again, but it was just the same. The race walker swung on, leaving the river to drive the girl under the bridge.

Now its black stone arches loomed overhead, and its gun-grey girders bent down like an iron mouth to eat her up. Waves ran ahead of her, disappearing out of sight, and the girl followed without a choice. There was nobody to help her. The treeless path stood empty. The cobbled tunnel stood empty. The girl was all alone. Whirlpools swirled around her. *There was no escaping.*

The waves dragged her down. Down and out, down and under, one minute there; and the next gone! The waves broke over her and the riverbed reached for her. Soft and silty, its tendrils of weed drew her down to where she'd never see the railway bridge again. Never have to cry for help again, nor cry for all the things she wouldn't see or do or be. All the things she wouldn't know – like who she was, and where she'd come from in the first place, and why she was ending up in the dark like this. Ending her story on chapter one.

'*I want to live!*' the girl cried out. 'It's just not fair! Give me a chance – that's all I ask!'

Just a chance.

Suddenly – as if the wanting it changed everything – the girl was up again. Nothing could keep her down, not even a silty riverbed, thick with weed. Stronger than whirlpools and stronger than waves, stronger than the railway bridge and stronger than anything, she was up like an arrow. She was reaching through the water, and in a seamless motion which saw her break its surface and head for the shore, she was fighting for her life. The iron girders, looming overhead, held no fears for her. And neither did the river. She knew that she could beat it. Every stroke was easy.

The bridge fell behind and the town drew close. The girl swam into the lee of a stone wharf where, amid a flotsam of old twigs and plastic bottles, her arms and legs finally gave out. The river deposited her on a small beach where she lay unable to move, her burst of energy gone as quickly as it had come.

She had landed at last. The girl looked down at herself. She wore a cotton shift-dress which clung, soaking wet, to her body, and a woollen blanket-thing, tied in a dripping knot under her chin. Her feet were blue, throbbing with the cold. Her hair was plastered over her eyes, but she didn't even have the energy to raise a hand and wipe it away.

She lay a long time without the energy to do anything. A walker looked down on her from the top of the wharf, then hurried on, tutting to himself at the antics of some people's children. The girl watched him disappear. He passed through an archway in the old town wall and started up a steep lane. Once he half-turned back, as if having second thoughts about leaving a child on the water's edge like that. Then he carried on – much to her relief.

He'd done what was needed, after all. Done all that *she* needed, at least! It means I can't be dreaming, the girl thought. This must be really happening. Someone's seen me at last!

A boy on the street

Phaze II walked through the town without anybody seeing him. He had the knack. He had it down to a fine art. He was a tall boy, and painfully thin, but nobody ever said, 'Who's that boy?' or, 'Shouldn't he be in school?' With his big black coat wrapped around him and his head kept down, nobody ever noticed him.

It was a cold day, winter on the way. Phaze II turned up his collar and cut through Old St Chad's Square on his way to the warmth and brightness of the shops on Pride Hill. Old St Chad's was a quiet square, where the town's colonels and bank managers lived out their retirements in tall town houses behind iron gates. In the centre of the square stood a grassy mound, and upon the mound stood the crumbling remains of an old church, its ruined walls open to the sky and to the crows which circled over it, waiting for the Chadman to feed them.

He was coming along now – an old man with matted hair, gnarled hands, torn clothes and bursting boots, settling on his usual bench with his bags of food around him. Phaze II passed him, and the crows came swooping down. They settled on the Chadman's head, shoulders, hands and lap. It was always like this with him, day in, day out, rain or shine. Phaze II carried on and the Chadman didn't see him. He never noticed anybody, preferring birds to human company.

Phaze II knew just how he felt. Leaving the Chadman whistling to the birds through his long parchment-yellow teeth, he slipped into an alley and started rummaging among the dustbins. In no time at all he'd found a couple of apples, a piece of cheese – which would be fine once the mould was scraped off – and half a jar of fermenting jam. These he tucked into the voluminous pockets of his coat, ready to move on for fresh pickings on Pride Hill. But a woman appeared, driving him back into the shadows.

She was dressed in a camel-coloured coat, and had a newspaper tucked under her arm like a weapon. For a moment Phaze II thought that she was coming for him, but she carried on without seeing him. She had something else in her sights.

The Chadman.

Phaze II watched the woman emerge into the square, heading straight for the old man, who was breaking up sandwiches for the birds. He hadn't seen her yet – but he soon would! She crossed the square, passed the old wall which held up the grassy mound and started up the path which ran across the top of it.

'Hey! You there!' she called. '*You!* Fellow! I've told you before! If you don't stop what you're doing, *right now*, I'll call the police!'

The Chadman carried on as if he hadn't heard, and Phaze II laughed into his collar. The idea that anybody – even the police – could change the Chadman's habits of a lifetime was amusing, to put it mildly. Phaze II watched the woman reach the bench and start chasing off the crows, shaking her newspaper at them. They made their getaway, flapping up on to the ruined

15

walls. The woman kept on at the Chadman, thrusting her newspaper into his face and shouting:

'A public nuisance, that's what you are! Spoiling our square with your filthy vermin! I'll have you put away if you don't stop feeding those crows! *Do you hear me?*'

The Chadman didn't hear her – or so it seemed, sitting staring through the woman as if she weren't there. More furious than ever, she grabbed his bacon sandwiches and threw them into a nearby bin, plucked bits of meat, bread and birdseed off the ground, and binned them too. All the while, he sat and let her do it. Even when she thrust her morning paper at him again, he sat and let her. His eyes glazed over as if he were away somewhere else, in a dream of his own making.

The woman snorted with the sheer frustration of fighting someone who wouldn't fight back, gave up at last and stomped away. Phaze II saw her coming, and melted between the dustbins, holding his breath until she'd swept past. He had a name for people like her. People who ran the town as if they owned it. Who had everything, but you never saw them sharing it. Who always knew what was good for everybody else, and were always telling everyone about it. People who had lives to live and families to go home to.

Scuds, he called them. *Stupid scuds*.

The woman disappeared, slamming a door behind her. Phaze II prepared to carry on at last to Pride Hill, but something new caught his attention. A girl came slinking into the square in a way that Phaze II recognised as his own. As different from the striding woman as anyone could be, she edged along the

16

grassy mound, moving through the shadows with her head down.

Phaze II watched her with more than curiosity. He knew everyone by sight, but the way he knew this girl was different. His hair stood up on end. *He had dreamt about her last night!* Watched her turn her head and seen her face as pale as a ghost's, even as he saw it now. Her eyes had been full of sadness and in the dream he'd wondered why she was so alone. Now he wondered again, taking in the soaking dress sticking to her body, and nothing else to keep her warm but some scrappy little shawl-thing tied around her neck.

Phaze II followed the girl, Pride Hill forgotten. She reached the end of the mound where he could see her face-on. There was something strange about her – something eerie. It wasn't just the dream making everything about her seem strange, and it wasn't that she plainly didn't know her way around. Even a couple of of BC boys picked up on it. Self-styled Border Commandos, normally so tough – and normally no friends to strangers – but they let her pass them on the square without a comment.

Phaze II waited until they'd gone, then followed the girl down Dogpole Alley. She reached the Bytheways' house, where their front door stood open and a sweater hung over the railings next to a garden fork and a row of potted plants. Nobody was in sight, but Phaze II could hear voices in the house.

So, it seemed, could the girl. She looked both ways and suddenly Phaze II knew what she was going to do. The voices started growing louder and, as if she realised how little time she had, the girl snatched the sweater and made off. She was very quick – but then she had to be. Only seconds later Mrs Bytheway emerged on to her front step, ready to get on with her potting.

'My sweater! *My birthday sweater!* It's gone!'

She ran back indoors, calling to her husband that her special present had been stolen. Phaze II seized his chance and hurried after the girl. But when he reached the end of the alley, emerging on to Pride Hill, she had already gone. Everybody else was there – shoppers, business people, Buddhist boys peddling tracts, farmers in town for market day, buskers and tourists. But no girl.

Phaze II searched for her, all the same. It was a small town and she couldn't have gone far. He scoured Pride Hill, all the way up to the high town cross at the top. Then he scoured the new shopping mall, slipping like a shadow up and down its levels and in and out of its glittering shops.

Then he looked in all the other places where he would have gone himself if he'd wanted to find a quiet corner to dry off. But the girl wasn't in the library in the hidden alcove between 'Local History' and 'Fishing'. She wasn't in the castle. She wasn't in any of the old churches. She wasn't in the bus station, or the railway station, or even sheltering in the warmth of the town museum. She wasn't in the all-day pubs in the wild west end of town, between the Welsh Bridge and the market hall. She wasn't even in the Mardol Cinema, disused and boarded up but easy to get into.

She wasn't anywhere. Or so it seemed.

Only at the end of the day did Phaze II catch sight of the girl again. He was down in the wild west end,

18

heading for the market to see if any of the traders had left anything behind. The market hall was locked but the girl stood outside its reinforced glass doors, gazing at her reflection. She was wearing the stolen sweater, which came down to her knees, and had found a pair of ill-fitting shoes to go with it. But it obviously wasn't them that the girl was looking at.

It was herself.

Phaze II stepped into the shadows so that the girl wouldn't see him. But he needn't have worried. There was something completely self-absorbed about the way she stared at her reflection. Something very odd. She wasn't preening. There wasn't anything self-pitying in her gaze. There wasn't even anything curious.

It was only later that Phaze II realised what it was. He was making his way up Pride Hill in the dark. The girl had long since gone again, melted into the night. All the shops were shuttered and only a few last workers were about, heading for the station while the town beggars called after them for small change.

Phaze II slipped past them all, in the shadows until he reached the bright lights of the shopping mall at the top of the hill. And suddenly there he was reflected in a window – a tall gangling boy in a flapping coat. He stared at himself and it dawned on him that the girl hadn't looked the way that he did, knowing what he'd find. She'd stared in the way people stared at strangers. As if she'd never seen that person reflected in the glass door.

Never seen herself before.

Phaze II hurried on, telling himself that it didn't matter what the girl had seen or known or thought. It had nothing to do with him. The first rule of life was not to get involved, and the second was *not to dream!*

He passed the high town cross and started down the road on the other side. Time was ticking by and soon the town's nightlife would begin. There'd be people on the streets again, especially in the wild west end and around the railway station. People full of drink and maybe even fight. It could get like that on a Friday night. Especially when the BC boys were in town.

Phaze II hurried on, pausing only to rifle through a final litter bin down by the railway station. Here he pulled out half a mega-pizza in a box and a crumpled bag of chips. It was a major haul. Marvelling at what people threw away, he carried on. Old Sabrina would be waiting, and she'd be hungry. She had ways of punishing him if he left her for too long. She wasn't easy, Old Sabrina, but who could blame her? She had no one else to depend on. Only him.

The sweetest music

The girl spent her first night in the old, disused Mardol Cinema. It took a while to get into, but was worth the effort when she found it dry and warm inside. Its emergency lighting system was still working and there were even chocolate bars to be found in the back of a cupboard. The floors were still carpeted, and she curled up beneath the empty screen, sleeping like the dead until daylight awoke her.

It came seeping through the cracks around the emergency exit, bringing no clues to the time of day. The clock had long since stopped, leaving cinema-time at an eternal midnight. The girl crept into the ladies' toilet – a marvel of dusty china basins, marble surrounds, shell-shaped lights and tall mirrors tinted pink. In these she could see her reflection again – a row of ragged girls with shoes too big to walk in comfortably. Her face was pinched, her hair a tangled mess and the grubby blanket, knotted under her chin, fit only to be thrown away.

But it was all the girl had brought with her. All she'd got, along with this reflection of a child she didn't know. She looked at her body with its thin arms, legs and chest. Who was she? Who and *what*? She didn't feel like a child inside herself – and yet why not?

She left the cinema the way that she'd entered, slipping between loose boards. Someone shouted,

'What d'you think you're doing?' and she ran off into a network of alleys. It was easy to lose herself. The town was like a maze. She rambled around, looking for clues to who she was and where she'd come from. She went down to the bus station, looking for destinations that might sound familiar. Did the same at the railway station. Looked at people's faces, wondering if she'd find somebody that she knew. Even stood in front of a television shop, waiting for a news item about a lost child – some frantic mother on the screen, calling for her daughter to come home.

But there was no news item, and night fell again. The girl headed back to the Mardol Cinema, but when she got there the boards had been renailed. What was she going to do? She tried the market hall, but it was locked for the night. Tried the shopping mall at the top of Pride Hill, but it was locked too. Tried the library, the castle and even the town museum. But everywhere was locked.

The girl ended up by the river, clambering beneath the castle wall, trying to find a way of getting in. Suddenly the ground slipped away beneath her. She hadn't realised how steep it was – and now it was too late. A landslide of stones and loose soil took hold of her and swept her down a steep bank to the wall which ran behind the river path. Along the top of it had been erected a barricade of iron bars, jagged bits of glass and barbed wire. And built above the wall, at right angles to it, stood the railway bridge.

Its top was lit by platform lights, shining green and orange through a row of arched window panes. But its underbelly was as dark as ever. The girl watched the river flowing under it out of sight. Above her, a voice announced that the train due on Platform Seven was going to be late. Beneath her, a little mist rose from the river and drifted into the tunnel, where a wall full of graffiti announced:

NO HOPE!

NO LIFE!

GOD IS DEAD!

DIE BLOODY WELSH!

DIE BLACKS!

BLOODY FAIRY POOFTERS, OUT OUT OUT!

BORDER COMMANDOS RULE!!!

The girl shivered at the words, painted black, each dripping letter thick with hate. She turned to get away, as if the hate were directed at her personally. But more stones and earth came slipping down and she found herself trapped, unable to go forwards, unable to go back. Scared, lost and cold, she started whimpering. All the questions that she'd asked herself during the day came tumbling out.

'*Why me?*' she asked again. 'What was I doing in that river? What am I doing here? Where have I come from? Where's my home? Where's my family? Why can't I remember anything? Do I have a mother? Do I have a story? Do I have *anybody* out there?'

Desperately the girl struggled to remember back beyond that first moment on the river when the mist had parted and there she was. But there were no answers beyond the mist. There were no memories. For all her trying, there was nothing. She held her head and rocked back and forth. *What was she going to do?* She didn't know. She tried not to think. Closed her eyes, tried not to move, but succeeded only in bringing down more stones and earth.

The girl cried out and a low note answered as if on cue. It came twisting through the darkness – a lonely sound which could have been anything from the nightly haunting of the town ghost to a train screeching overhead. At first the girl couldn't make it out, but then she heard another note, and another. And then she realised. It was a tune.

A stupid tune! The girl almost laughed out loud. What she wanted was her memory, to rescue her with answers. But what she got was music instead! She looked around, trying to see where it was coming from, but the river path stood empty, and so did the railway tunnel. Nobody was here to play to her, but she could hear the tune all the same.

The girl listened to it, reluctant at first, but slowly lulled despite herself. How could it be otherwise? The tune sang out as if it were a living thing, soaring and swooping among the girders of the railway bridge, echoing up to its black stone arches and rolling across the river like mist. And its notes were words, and every one of them a song of secret comfort.

'You're fine,' it sang out. '*Really. Fine. You're brave and strong and where you should be. There's nothing* to be frightened of. *Everything is just fine. Trust me.*'

And the girl did! The notes seeped into her like an enchantment, and suddenly she *was* fine! She knew she was, just like the tune said. She didn't feel sorry for herself any more. She didn't feel frightened. She felt safe.

For the first time, the girl noticed how beautiful the night had become. She looked around her, and the air was glittering with frost. The bridge wasn't dark any more, but sparkling with jewels of ice. The stones and earth around her were covered with diamonds, and the glass along the top of the wall shone with bright spangles.

It was a jewel of a night, and the river formed its backdrop, as black as polished ebony. The girl found a pile of frozen leaves and lay her head upon them. The mist came off the river and wrapped itself around her, as soft and warm as a fur stole. Tomorrow she might wake up frozen to the bone, but tonight everything was *just fine.*

The girl closed her eyes and let the sweetest music pour through her mind, whispering that she wasn't lonely, lost, cold and wretched – whispering that she had a home somewhere, and she would find it one day soon.

Her breath came slow and calm and even. The frayed edge of her little knotted blanket lay beneath her cheek. Her dress clung to her body, freezing over. Her stolen sweater froze too. But as she fell asleep, she felt brave and strong and safe.

Hallowe'en

Bentley packed away the saxophone and left his hideaway under the railway bridge. It wasn't really late, but his mother would begin to worry if he didn't get back home. He emerged from the tunnel, sorry as always to be leaving behind his secret concert hall, with its wonderful echoey acoustics. There was nowhere like it in town, not even the music hall or the perfect amphitheatre of the Quarry Park. Not even the town churches, where he sometimes played the organ and his father rang the bells.

He headed for home, reliving his evening's playing. He had come here countless times before to practise his favourite pieces, confident that the bridge's acoustics would cover his mistakes. But tonight there had been no mistakes. Music had poured through him like a river on its way somewhere. He'd played like an angel and he knew it, blowing up into the arches and girders of the railway bridge, and down through the mist. If Dad had heard him playing like that, he would have been proud. And if he'd only played like that at home, Mum would have been less likely to scold him for wasting time and not getting on with his homework.

Bentley reached the archway in the old town wall, stopped to take a final glance back at the bridge, then turned up the lane for home. Somewhere in the town, a clock struck eleven. It was later than he had realised, and he broke into a trot which didn't stop until he reached Pride Hill. Here the wide sweep of the town's main shopping street was empty save for a lone cellist sitting in a doorway playing to himself.

At the sight of the cellist, dressed in dinner jacket and bow tie, Bentley would have turned back and gone another way. But he wasn't quick enough. The cellist looked up. On the ground in front of him was a black top hat in which lay his evening's takings. Pinned to the hat were the words JULIAN BOYD-WIBBLER, FIRST CELLIST WITH THE PENGWERN CONSERVATOIRE. *Fallen Upon Hard Times.*

It was meant to be a joke, but when the cellist was your father and some days he was PANCHO THE PAN-PIPE-PLAYING PERUVIAN, *Fallen Upon Hard Times*, and sometimes PADDY MC-BY-THE-WAY, UILLEAN PIPE MASTER, *Fallen Upon the Potato Famine* – there for all the town to see beneath the hats as Mr Bytheway, the music teacher – it wasn't very funny.

'Evening, Bentley,' Dad said, continuing the fast movement of a cello concerto without dropping a note. 'What are you doing with my saxophone?'

'What are *you* doing, more to the point?' Bentley said, blushing and thrusting his father's saxophone behind his back. 'You know how mad Mum gets when you go out busking! Especially on a night like this, with not a soul about to fill your hat!'

They both looked at the pennies in the bottom of the hat. A cold wind was blowing up the hill, and Bentley shivered. Dad stopped playing at last, and the sudden silence was eerie. He started packing up.

'Your mum says busking doesn't pay, but we'll show her one day,' he said, pocketing the pennies in the top hat. He winked at Bentley.

Bentley winked back. The two of them walked home together, hunched against the wind. It was nearly Hallowe'en and the shop windows were full of witches' masks and leering orange pumpkins. The streetlamps had been smashed in Dogpole Alley, and they had to crunch over broken glass to get up the front steps.

'It's always the same, this time of year,' Dad complained. 'Hallowe'en seems to bring out the worst in people. Broken glass and stolen sweaters. All tricks and no treats!'

They slipped into the house, shutting the door quietly as if they could sneak in without Mum noticing. Dad stopped to store the instruments in the downstairs room he called 'the music school', and Bentley hurried upstairs hoping that Mum would be in bed. But she was still up in the living room, sitting at her sewing machine with an eye on the clock.

'Where have you been?' she said when he came in. 'Busking with your father? No, don't tell me! You should be working for good grades, not playing on the streets and making fools of yourselves!'

Dad followed Bentley into the room. 'Once you used to love this fool for his music,' he said.

'I loved you for yourself, not *Julian Boyd-Wibbler*!' Mum said.

'You wouldn't say that if you knew how much he's made!'

Dad tipped out his evening's pennies and Mum looked at them and burst out laughing. She shook her head as if she knew she couldn't win, put aside her sewing and they all went to bed.

In the morning Bentley woke up late for school. The

alarm clock lay across the room where he had thrown it. Mum had already gone to work, and Dad was nowhere to be seen. A note on the table informed Bentley that if he wanted cereal, he'd have to nip out and buy milk.

Bentley didn't bother with the cereal, or any other breakfast, and hurried off to school knowing he'd be late. He forgot the only bit of homework that he'd managed to get done, and his physics teacher made him stay for detention at the end of the day. When he finally came out of school, it was getting dark. He trailed through town feeling sorry for himself. He was starving hungry, having forgotten lunch as well as breakfast, but knew that when he got home he'd have to face Mum, who would have been phoned about the detention.

So he drifted round the town, putting off the evil moment by mooching round the shops. Finally they began to close and Pride Hill started emptying. The newspaper sellers shut up for the night and even the town beggars disappeared for a quiet break before the night's trade.

Bentley turned for home at last. What else could he do? Only a few moments ago the town had thronged with life, but now everything seemed quiet and eerie. In Dogpole Alley, the streetlamps were still broken, and in the darkness he imagined ghosts and ghouls ready to jump out. This was Hallowe'en night, after all! Not that Bentley believed in ghosts and ghouls, of course!

All the same, he made a quick dash for it, getting halfway down the alley before the BC boys started coming the other way. *The BC boys* – far more trouble than ghosts and ghouls! Bentley headed for his front door, and the boys came whooping down the alley, dressing in Hallowe'en masks and chasing somebody. Bentley fumbled for his front-door key, pitying whoever it might be, but telling himself that it had nothing to do with him. After all, he knew what Border Commandos were like! Some of them were still in school, and if you dared to get in their way they could make your life a total misery.

Bentley's key wasn't in his pockets, so he started on his school bag. The BC boys' quarry had nearly reached him, and they were right behind. He could hear their panting, and see them in a solid mass, yelling, 'Trick or treat!' through their masks at what was nothing but a little girl.

Just a child, half their size!

Bentley couldn't quite believe that even BC boys would waste their time on a little girl. He stared at them contemptuously. The girl drew level with him. Her shoes were too big for her and she kept tripping over. Briefly he caught a glimpse of her white face, then she turned towards the Seventy Steps, which led down from the alley to the bus station. *The Seventy Steps*, where anything could happen in the darkness! And it often did.

Behind her in the alley, the BC boys howled with delight. They'd got her now! They knew they had! They headed for the steps as well, devils in plastic masks – and if anybody was going to stop them, they'd have to do it now!

Bentley didn't even pause to think about it. He shouted at the girl. The BC boys would get him for it, but he did it all the same.

'Not down there! This way!'

30

The girl turned, saw Bentley waving at her, and seized her chance. She whirled about and leapt up the steps before the boys could grab her. Bentley found his key as if by magic. He unlocked the door and the two of them tumbled inside.

The BC boys howled with rage. 'Witch! Bitch! Little gypo vampire-girl! Out, out, out!' they yelled.

The girl backed down the hall, her eyes two perfect moons, round and shining with fear. Bentley bolted the door, glad that it was old and solid. He leant against it, unable to stop shaking as he waited for the BC boys to charge.

But as if they knew that they were beaten for today, the BC boys gave up. Bentley heard a last few yells, then silence settled over Dogpole Alley. Bentley closed his eyes, wondering what had come over him, and knowing that the BC boys would make him pay. And when he opened them again, there was the girl, staring at him.

She wore nothing that would keep her warm, just a lacy sweater which wasn't really thick enough, and a little ragged blanket-thing knotted under her chin. Her hair looked as if it hadn't been washed for weeks, and her face was stretched to breaking point by sheer exhaustion. Bentley could see it in her eyes, along with the fear. Fear of him as well as everybody else. Fear of everything, including this dark, silent house.

'I won't hurt you. I only want to help you. I'm not like them,' Bentley said.

He unbolted the front door, as if to say that she was free to go. But she looked at him, and suddenly he realised that she had nowhere else. And when he started up the stairs, she followed him.

Part Two
River Matters

Part Two
River Fortress

Abren

The boy turned on the light as they started up the stairs, revealing a worn strip of carpet and a high, moulded plaster ceiling, a row of hooks on the wall and coats piled on them. The girl followed him up into the winding darkness. They passed a single door on the first floor, then carried on to the top of the house. Here, beneath sloping eaves, she found a succession of rooms nestled together. Some were bedrooms. One was a junk room. One was a bathroom. And one was the boy's room, his name, BENTLEY, stencilled on the door.

Behind this door, the girl found a clutter of shelves, desk, chests of drawers and a bed, all tucked between a dusty skylight and an old oak frame. Books lined the frame, which doubled as a shelf. A pile of old records, mostly out of their sleeves, lay in the corner, and photographs of musicians in nightclubs hung on the walls.

The girl looked at the photographs while the boy, Bentley, threw his school bag on the bed. She wanted to thank him, but didn't know where to start. He pulled off his jacket and put on a record. Immediately a voice called from downstairs.

'Bentley, is that you?'

Bentley pulled a face. He didn't say anything, but led the girl back down to a first-floor room with tall windows looking out on Dogpole Alley. At one end a

35

collection of armchairs, a sofa and a TV set were arranged around a fireplace. At the other stood a cooker and a washing machine, workbenches and a sink, an old dresser and a huge kitchen table.

Between the two ends, facing the door, sat a big bony woman with a straight face, high, flat cheeks and a square box of fringed hair. She looked just like Bentley and had to be his mother. Around her were spread a tailor's dummy, a pile of paper patterns and a heap of cloth which went whizzing past her under the needle of her sewing machine.

She raised her head as Bentley came in. Started on about detention and coming home late – then saw the girl behind him.

'Mum, this is ...' Bentley broke off. Looked at the girl.

'*Abren,*' she said, blushing as she plucked the first name that came to her out of thin air. 'My name's Abren.'

'Abren,' Bentley's mother said, looking the girl up and down – and finishing at her sweater.

The girl shuffled awkwardly, wondering if something was the matter.

'We met down in the alley,' Bentley said. 'The BC boys were chasing her – you must have heard them!'

It seemed his mother had. 'So *that* was what was going on!' she said, looking at the girl in a whole new light. 'You can stay for tea, if you want. You look like you could do with it. Bentley'll show you to the bathroom and you can get yourself clean. Don't take too long, though, because tea's late already. By the way, I'm Mrs Bytheway!'

It was obviously her idea of a joke, but Bentley

groaned and said he'd had enough of that at school, thank you very much! He showed Abren the bathroom, where she scrubbed her face and hands, brushed a few tangles out of her hair and stared long at her face. Mrs Bytheway broke in upon her thoughts by calling her down. She returned to find a man, in corduroy trousers held up with braces, laying the table. He was Mr Bytheway, he said. 'But you can call me Fee. Everybody does. Come and sit down.'

The girl sat where she was bidden, between Bentley and his mother. They talked about their day, including Bentley's latest reason for detention. Their voices droned over the girl's head, and she ate in silence. When she'd finished, she licked her plate. Everybody stared at her, but she didn't notice.

'Here, have some more,' said Fee.

He pushed the bright enamel stewing pot across the table, and the girl helped herself to more stew and dumplings. She hadn't realised that she was hungry until now. She licked the second plate clean and would have had a third if there had been one. Fee cut up some bread and she scoffed it down. He brought a chocolate pudding out of the fridge and she scoffed down more than her fair share, groaning with delight over its chocolate sauce.

While she ate a second helping of this too, and licked her pudding plate, a conversation sprang up about the BC boys, and whether the police did enough to protect the town at night. Mrs Bytheway was in favour of closed circuit TV but Fee said it would make no difference. He turned to the girl, as if to see what she thought, but tiredness had overwhelmed her. Her face lay on the table within reach of the last of the chocolate sauce, but too exhausted to do anything about it.

'We've got to get that poor child back home!' Mrs Bytheway said.

'She hasn't got a home – can't you see that?' Bentley said.

'Of course she's got a home! Everybody has,' Mrs Bytheway said.

'No, they haven't,' Bentley said. 'At least, not her. I mean, look how pale she is. And look how she eats. And the way she watches us, as if she doesn't know if she can trust us? She's been living rough – it's obvious!'

When the girl woke up again, the argument had been settled. Bentley had unfolded a sofa bed in front of the fire, and Fee was making it up with crisp white pillows and bedcovers. They were keeping her for the night and would 'sort her out in the morning', according to Mrs Bytheway. She got the girl to her feet, walked her to the sofa bed and forced her into pyjamas, carting off her clothes, declaring, 'If I do nothing else tonight, I'm going to wash these filthy things.'

Among them was the sweater, which she muttered over, calling it her 'poor, ruined birthday present'.

The girl fell back to sleep, realising for the first time that this was the very house from which she'd snatched the sweater. But she was too tired to care, and there was nothing she could do about it anyway. The curtains were drawn, the sheets smelt sweet and the crackle of the fire was hypnotic. Her stomach was full of stew, dumplings and chocolate pudding, and she fell asleep again. She didn't hear her dirty clothes being piled into the washing machine. Didn't wake up when a hot-water bottle was tucked under her feet, nor when the Bytheways went up to bed, turning out the lights.

She fell into a drowning deep sleep until morning, and awoke at first light. Someone was moving across the floor. She heard them drop something on her bed, then creep away. Through slits of eyes, she saw that it was Mrs Bytheway. She left the room, closing the door behind her and, a moment later, closing the front door too.

Her footsteps clattered down the alley, and the girl sat up. The fire was cold, and grey light came prying through the cracks between the curtains, dimly revealing a pile of ironed and folded clothes at the bottom of the bed. The girl took a closer look and found that they included the sweater, folded up for her, an unexpected gift. But before she had the time to appreciate it, the girl noticed her blanket too.

Her special woolly blanket, which she'd brought with her from her old life! The girl grabbed it and rubbed its feathery edge against her cheek, relieved that though it smelt of washing powder, it still felt like the same old blanket. Then, holding it in her arms, she fell back to sleep.

Only when she awoke later, in the full light of day, did she realise that the blanket wasn't quite the same, after all. She lifted her head, and there upon her pillow was a mass of colour, all the grime washed away. No longer was the blanket a dull uniform grey. It was covered with embroidery. Birds flew over it, and flowers blossomed. Mountains rose upon its soft woollen cloth, and rivers ran away from them.

Woodlands stood tall, and the sky above them was as blue as skies can only be in dreams.

In astonishment the girl looked at a row of white swans, a gang of men towing a square-sailed boat and a palace in an embroidered town with trees and roads and little houses. Underneath them all, five letters had been embroidered with gold thread. They ran along the bottom of the blanket, where the river turned to sea. The girl touched each of them in turn. And even then she couldn't quite believe that here, as if embroidered for her especially, was the very name she'd chosen for herself:

A B R E N

St Chad's crypt

Abren didn't need to put on her freshly ironed clothes in order to feel dressed. She had a name – and not one plucked out of thin air. A real name. *Abren.* She snuggled back down in the bed, clutching her little blanket as if she'd never let it go. She mightn't know what she'd been doing on that river; mightn't know where she came from, whether she had a family or a home. But she knew this much. *She was Abren.*

Fee came downstairs and started making breakfast, singing to himself. Bentley clattered down to join him, all dressed up for school. How was Abren? he wanted to know. Had she slept? Was she all right? And, most importantly, was she going to stay with them?

'We could put her in the boxroom,' he said, glancing at the figure in the sofa bed, pretending to be sleeping. 'I've always wanted a brother or sister, and Mum's always going on about needing women in the family, and—'

'Don't be silly, Bentley. We've got to take her home,' Fee said.

'*But she hasn't got a home!*' Bentley said.

'She must have someone somewhere, Bentley! She isn't just a puppy we've picked up on the streets!'

'I don't care what you say. I want her to stay!'

The toaster popped and the kettle boiled. Fee went one way and Bentley the other, and only later did they return to the subject.

'She can't stay,' Fee said. 'I'm sorry, Bentley. But you can't just keep people like that! She's someone's child. She *has* to be. She has a home somewhere, and we've got to take her back. Either that or we'll have to call the police!'

They finished their breakfasts and Bentley left for school, pausing only to take a look at Abren, who was still pretending to be asleep.

'I'll never speak to you or Mum again if you call the police!'

Abren lay still until he'd gone, shortly followed by Fee. Then she leapt up, grabbed her clothes and pulled them on as fast as she could. She didn't want to be the reason for Bentley's family never speaking again. But she didn't want them calling the police, and neither did she want them finding her family.

Grabbing her embroidered blanket, she bolted down the stairs and out through the front door. For all her questions about herself, she didn't know whether she wanted answers after all. None of them could tell her why she felt a stranger in her own body, or why everybody stared at her as if she were different, or why she couldn't remember anything.

Abren wandered round the town in a dull, strange daze. Every time she passed a newspaper hoarding she looked away. Yesterday she'd hoped to find a headline about a missing child, but not today. Every time a bus drove by she hoped its journey destination scroll wouldn't ring a bell.

As the day wore on, people started noticing a little girl who seemed to have nowhere to go. Shoppers turned and stared at her as she went by. News-sellers said that, yes, they'd seen her on Pride Hill several times today – and yesterday as well, come to think of it. And, no, they didn't know who she was.

Feeling eyes following her wherever she went, Abren returned to the river. She rested in a shed, among a pile of tennis nets, until a class of schoolgirls and their teacher came along. Sheltered under a bandstand while a crowd of boys and girls flirted overhead, and even fell asleep down there until a dog chased her out.

By now it was getting dark and she returned into town, skulking in alleys and hiding behind rubbish bins until the shops shut and the streets fell empty. Then, cold and hungry, she trailed through the main streets of the town, with no clear idea of where she was heading or what she should do. Drawing level with the market hall she noticed a tall, thin boy in a flapping coat methodically combing through the rubbish bins, looking for food. She hid in the shadows until he'd gone, then tried the same trick. But he'd left nothing edible in any of them, just a pile of empty boxes, some old newspapers and a bunch of dog-eared roses.

The girl hauled these out. Some were dead, but some weren't too bad. She straightened the cellophane around them, fished out their plastic bow and stuck it back on. Then she took the flowers round to Dogpole Alley and left them poking through the Bytheway's letter box. The house lights were out and the alley was dark. She hurried away, hoping that the flowers would thank them for their kindness and for the sweater. Hoping, too, that they wouldn't mind about her running off. That they'd have forgotten her already, and were out somewhere having fun.

She reached the end of the alley and suddenly it felt lonely, imagining other people having fun. A bitter wind blew across Old St Chad's Square, rattling the windows of the tall town houses, their curtains drawn against the night. Abren turned her face away from them and their little bits of light, and started round the square, following the old wall which held up the mound.

Halfway round she came upon an iron-grilled gate, leading to a dark place which could have been an old church crypt, or maybe a store attached to one of the houses. It looked warm down there out of the wind, and perhaps it could be a shelter for the night. Abren decided to investigate. She slipped through the grill and stumbled down a flight of steps. The darkness rose to greet her like an old friend. Overcome with weariness, she edged her way forwards, looking for a place to lay down her head until finally she struck a far wall.

She started working along it, feeling her way into some sort of niche, thinking that she'd found her shelter for the night. But then she sensed something in front of her. *Something warm*. She couldn't see what it was, but suddenly she caught a whiff of something pungent and unpleasant.

Abren turned away, trying not to gag. She put out a hand – and *touched something clammy!* She spun around with a cry, hit the wall on one side of her, bounced off it and stumbled backwards through a darkness which seemed to last for ever. Finally she fell against the steps. She scrambled up them and squeezed through the iron-grilled gate. And never had a night in a lonely square in an empty town felt so good! The wind was fresh, not cold. It wasn't bitter any more. It just felt good and alive.

Abren crossed the square, scarcely knowing where she was going – until she bumped into someone coming the other way.

'It *was* you! Mum and Dad thought that kids were mucking about. But the moment I saw the flowers, I just knew!'

The someone was Bentley, clutching the roses. He hugged Abren with relief, and she burst into tears. She felt a fool, but couldn't stop.

'It's all right,' Bentley said, letting her go as if he felt a fool too. '*It's all right*. We've found you again – that's what matters. We never thought we would. We'd almost given up. But now we can go home.'

He turned towards Dogpole Alley, but Abren hung back. Home, she thought? What home? The wind blew at her, but she couldn't move.

Bentley turned back. 'We can't just stay here,' he said.

'I can't go with you. Not unless you promise,' Abren said.

'Promise what?'

'No looking for my family. No police. *And no questions asked!*'

No questions asked

They kept their promise, but what they thought about it, Abren could only guess. She became a member of the family, and none of them asked her anything. She moved into the boxroom next to Bentley. Fee emptied it out, and they all helped do it up, providing everything a proper bedroom needed, from pictures on the walls to chests of drawers and hand-me-down clothes. Fee gave Abren a stack of books; some of them were old and boring-looking, but he said she should never judge a book by its cover. Bentley brought her a cassette player with a broken lid, and a pile of music tapes. Mrs Bytheway bought her hairbrushes and washing things, nightdresses, socks and brand-new underwear.

'If anybody asks,' she said, 'I'm your Aunty Mena, and you're our niece from away, come to stay. And if there's ever anything you want to tell us – anything at all – then our door's always open. But in your own time, of course. When you're ready and not before. *Only please don't run away again!*'

It was the last word on the subject – at least for now. The nearest Mena came to raising it was to leave the phone by Abren's bed, just in case she wanted to make a call, and a blank postcard as well, in case she wanted to post it to put someone's mind at rest. A stamp was stuck on it, and Abren spent restless hours wondering what she ought to do with it.

In the end, guessing that Mena was the one whose mind most needed putting at rest, she got up early, went out and posted the card. She left it blank save for the stamp, but at least she could say she'd done it, if she was asked. Then she hurried back to Dogpole Alley, relieved to get inside and close the door. Outside, her questions clamoured to get at her, but inside she was safe. She was one of the family. A cousin from away. *Abren Bytheway.*

Days passed by, turning into weeks. Autumn turned to winter. Have I really been here a week? Abren thought. Then, two weeks, is it really? Then, a month – surely not? She lived in Dogpole Alley as if the world beyond it simply wasn't there. The house felt like a fortress, high above the river, buried among the streets and alleys in the centre of the town. She felt safe within it, never going out. Here there were no BC boys to chase her. No Seventy Steps to draw her down them at her peril. No days spent wandering around, trying to avoid attention. No nights spent wondering where to lay her head.

And here there was no river, bearing questions for which Abren had no answers. Questions which she refused to think about, because *no questions asked* was the order of the day. Instead she buried herself in the routines of her new family's life, watching Bentley going to school, Fee working with his pupils in the 'music school' and Mena going out every morning, only to return home after lunch and get on with her second occupation – dressmaking.

It was the ritual of their lives. Fee went out busking at night, with ever-changing instruments and in matching costumes. Mena fussed over Abren, channelling her worries into making sure she kept her teeth clean, her hair untangled and she ate. And Bentley did his homework, at least when he had to, dreaming of Christmas and the end of term.

It was getting closer every day, freezing rain beating down Dogpole Alley and decorations lighting Pride Hill. But they didn't lure Abren. Even standing at the window watching passers-by with bulging bags of presents didn't stir her. The world beyond the windows was like the world inside the television screen. It might be real, but not real enough to touch!

One day, standing at the window, Abren heard Fee and Mena on the front step, locked in argument. Christmas was to blame, and so was money. Mena wanted Fee to stop making a fool of himself. *Using carols as a meal ticket* was how she described it. Fee said beggars couldn't be choosers – and she flew at him.

'We wouldn't have to beg if you'd only get a proper job!'

'I don't beg – *I busk*.'

'That's what you call it!'

'I call it an honourable profession, and an ancient one too! Hawkers and buskers have always been a part of life on Pride Hill! They've been here since the dawn of time!'

'I don't care about the dawn of time! This is the modern world. *A world that costs!*'

Far from giving up, Fee doubled his busking efforts. Night after night, rain or clear, he was out there on the hill. It was a busy time for all of them. Mena doubled her efforts too, her tailor's dummy up to its neck in office-party frocks. Even Bentley found himself caught up in Christmas preparations, staying late for rehearsals of the school pantomime, in which he was lumbered with the role of Chief Executive of Santa's Toyland.com

He pleaded with Abren to come and see it – and she said that she would. But on the night she cried off. She was feeling sick, she said. And maybe the thought of leaving her fortress did really make her feel sick, but the more important truth was that she had some Christmas preparations of her own, and wanted to get on with them.

So, when they'd all gone out, Abren settled down to make a Christmas present for Bentley, Fee and Mena, stealing a corner of party-frock cloth and a couple of skeins of embroidery silk, and starting to stitch a picture of birds and flowers, copied from her comfort blanket. When Fee and Mena came in, teasing Bentley over his success, Abren hid away her handiwork.

From then on, however, every time she was alone she did some more – stitching as fast as she could because Christmas was drawing close. And with its bustle of excitement came unexpected fears. What would Christmas Day bring for Abren Bytheway, playing the part of an ordinary girl in an ordinary family? What memories and questions would it trigger?

Abren felt the tension building up – not just in her, but in Mena too.

When Fee brought in a tree for them to decorate, Mena said that the real star of Christmas wasn't made of tinsel, it was made of openness and trust. She looked at Abren as she said it, and Abren blushed.

Then, the next day, Christmas Eve, busy cooking everybody's favourites while Fee was out dressed up as Santa Claus on Pride Hill, she suddenly said, 'I wonder what your mother's doing right now. I wonder if she's missing you.'

Again she looked at Abren, as if blaming her for something. Abren flushed. She didn't say a thing, but when Mena turned to get something out of the oven, she slipped from the room, stumbling down the stairs with tears pricking her eyes. If it hadn't been for bumping into Bentley, on his way to market for their last-minute shopping, she didn't know what she would have done.

'Do you want to come?' he said, as if he could tell that something was wrong.

In the end, Abren was glad that she said yes. Down in the market – surrounded by a sea of turkeys, geese, wild hares, pheasants, partridges, huge slabs of pork and rolls of beef – it was impossible to think of anything but Christmas. Bentley dragged her between stalls of fruit, vegetables, nuts, home-made pork pies, home-cured bacon, jars of fat olives, slabs of pinky salmon, floury loaves of bread and twists of rolls, new-laid free-range ducks' and hens' and quails' eggs, and every sort of cheese that Abren could have imagined, from plain to holey and from starkest white to pinks and greens and oranges.

He did the shopping, and Abren helped carry the bags, trying to keep up with him. The market hall was heaving, everyone pushing and shoving, and in the crowd they became separated. Abren found herself wandering on her own down an avenue of flower stalls. At the end she saw a boy who she thought was

Bentley. But when he started coughing, she realised that he was someone else.

She fixed her eyes on him – a tall, thin boy with a big black coat, looking at her as if they'd met before. And he looked familiar to Abren too. But only later did she realise that he was the boy she'd seen going through the bins. The one who'd left the roses behind, but no food.

She turned away, bumped into the real Bentley and followed him home. Here Mena said that she was sorry for her quick tongue, and gave Abren a hug. Abren said it didn't matter, but she lay awake that night, thinking about her mother. What *was* she doing now? Was she missing Abren? Was she out there somewhere, dressed as Santa and filling Abren's stocking just in case she came home? Was she looking for her – looking even now, in the middle of the night?

Abren closed her eyes and tried to sleep. But her questions wouldn't leave her alone, and finally she got up and went downstairs. In the kitchen everything was ready for the morning, a testimony to Mena's hard work. The turkey waited for its chestnut-and-pork stuffing. The Christmas pudding sat with a cloth tied over it. The Brussels sprouts had been peeled and left to soak in a pan. And even a glass of sherry had been left on the table, with a box of chocolates bearing a note to *'Santa@Toyland.com – from your Chief Executive!!'*

Abren opened up the luscious chocolates which the note said were *'for all the busy elves who work so hard to wrap up Santa's presents'*. The other elves weren't around to share them, and suddenly Abren couldn't resist making a start. And once started, there was no stopping! Champagne truffles. Chocolate fudge. Hazelnut pralines. Cherry kirsch. Butternut delights. Mocha marzipan. Whisky cream. Orange fizzes.

Abren ate until her stomach heaved. Until the box was empty and she felt too sick to think about her mother or anything else. Then she went to bed, knowing that the chocolates had done the trick. *No questions asked* was still the order of the day!

Bentley's carol

Abren came downstairs on Christmas morning to find everybody teasing everybody else about the chocolates. As soon as she appeared, they turned on her with the empty box. It had to be her, they said. She was the chocoholic in the family – the one who'd licked her pudding plate clean on that first day, and had been at the chocolate ever since!

'*I'm* not the one who spends his dinner money on chocolate bars!' Abren teased back. 'And I'm not the one who keeps a secret store in her sewing-machine drawer!'

Everybody laughed. Abren changed the subject by showing them all the contents of her stocking, and Bentley showed his too, marvelling at the way that Santa always managed to squeeze in useful things like socks and soap.

Fee went to church to ring the Christmas-morning bells. Mena remained behind, bustling between vegetables and sauces, the fridge and the cooker, the freezer, the sherry bottle and the phone. She chased Abren and Bentley away from the presents under the tree, persuading them to wait until after lunch with bribes of chocolate, cakes, biscuits, dates and nuts. All the while she kept nipping at the sherry and by the time that Fee came home, she was singing. Fee said she was drunk, and she said perhaps she was, but that she worked 'like a skivvy' all year long and deserved to be excessive once in a while.

It was a day for all of them to be excessive. Mince pies arrived before lunch, washed down with yet more sherry and cheap, fizzy wine. Still more chocolates followed the mince pies, and lunch followed the chocolates in a feast to which there seemed no ending. Soon, half the turkey was a carcass, the Christmas pudding had disappeared, the wine bottle was empty and the trifle was reduced to lumps of jelly floating in a small custard pond. A mountain of dishes sat piled in the sink, 'to do later' as Fee put it when Mena looked at him in vain hope.

It was time for presents, he said, not washing-up. They settled round the tree and Fee switched on the fairy lights. Bentley handed round the packages, and books and music tapes, a pair of football boots, a pile of silver jewellery, yet more chocolate, sweaters, games, stockings, perfume, soap and socks started falling out.

Abren opened a book called *Homecoming*, about a girl called Dicey who'd lost her mother and didn't have a home. Fee had inscribed the inside cover with the words, *'I thought you might enjoy this story. Tell me what you think.'* Then Abren opened another package which contained a thick red coat, made on Mena's sewing machine. Along with it went a woolly hat with flaps, and gloves with furry trims.

Fee had a hat as well, to keep him warm when he went out busking. He also received a huge biography of his all-time favourite cellist, Paul Tortelier.

But Bentley's was the biggest present of them all.

Fee went downstairs to the 'music school' and brought up something encased in blankets because he'd forgotten to buy any wrapping paper. It was a brand-new saxophone, golden and gleaming! Everybody stared at it in astonishment. Bentley turned bright red.

'Now you don't have to borrow mine any more,' Fee said.

'But we can't afford it!' Mena said.

'Of course we can – what d'you think I've been playing for all this time on Pride Hill?' Fee said.

He beamed. Point scored. Mena flushed. Abren could see that she wanted to be pleased, but that something was eating away at her.

'It's very nice, I'm sure,' she said, managing a tight smile.

'Bentley deserves it. He deserves the best. He's got real talent, and *he works hard*,' Fee said.

He beamed at Bentley, full of pride. But Mena flushed as if she'd been stung.

'Unlike some of us, I suppose!' she said, 'who don't deserve to have hundreds of pounds spent on us, not even for the luxury of a *new dish-washing machine*!'

For a moment there was silence. Maybe it was the drink that had done it. Fee said something very quiet about spoiling things, and Mena snapped back that the only person being spoiled was Bentley. Bentley clutched his brand-new saxophone, and if it hadn't been for Abren and her present it wouldn't have felt like Christmas any more.

Suddenly she saw where she had put it, right at the back of the tree behind everything else. She pulled it out and gave it to Mena.

'It's nothing really,' she said, hoping that it would cheer things up. 'I just wanted to thank you for everything.'

Mena took the present and looked ashamed, as if she had forgotten all about Christmas, and here it was back again. She opened it up and Abren's little piece of embroidery fell out. She hadn't thought to iron it or sew a hem, but it didn't matter.

'Oh, Abren!' Mena said. 'This is beautiful. Wherever did you get it?'

'I made it,' Abren said.

'You *made* it?'

Mena stared at the little trees and flowers, the birds and the river, all beautifully stitched. She stared for so long that Abren began to shift awkwardly, wondering if she was going to be told off for stealing the silks and the little bit of cloth. But then Mena leant across and gave her a big hug.

Suddenly it was Christmas again. They sat around the tree, and Mena asked Bentley to play some carols on his new saxophone. It was as if she wanted to show that there were no hard feelings. Fee started reading his Paul Tortelier book, and Mena picked up Abren's embroidery and came and sat with her.

'Whoever taught you to sew fairy stitches like these?' she said. 'A young girl like you – I can hardly believe it!'

Abren shrugged. She didn't know.

'Was it your mother?' Mena said.

Her mother again. Abren looked away. On the other side of the room Bentley had given up on the carols and was composing tunes of his own. His eyes were closed, and he was playing as if for himself alone. Playing the sweetest notes on his brand-new saxophone, unaware that everybody was listening. Mena sighed as if she'd never known that her Bentley could play like that. Fee beamed with pride. Bentley nursed the saxophone in his arms, coaxing out a tune as if it were a carol composed especially for today.

It rose to the ceiling and rolled across the room. Suddenly Abren recognised what he was playing. *It was 'her' tune!* Her tune again, whispering that she mustn't worry about her mother and about who had taught her fairy stitches. Whispering that she mustn't worry about anything. That she was *just fine*.

Abren listened, mesmerised. She looked at Mena, smiling despite everything. Looked at Fee as he hummed along. Looked at Bentley blowing as if he'd never stop. And suddenly she knew that she had to leave them! She couldn't keep on like this, playing at happy families. She wasn't Abren Bytheway. She was another girl. There were things out there beyond the fortress walls of Dogpole Alley that she'd come here to this town to do. Things she'd come to find out. And the tune was calling her to find them. To ask the questions, and to move on.

Abren pulled her little comfort blanket around her shoulders, left the others sitting in the semi-darkness and slipped down into Dogpole Alley. The streets were cold, but the tune had made her strong enough to face them. With it still ringing in her ears, she left the alley and strode across Old St Chad's Square, passing the iron-grilled gate and following the road round to the Water Lane. She was going to the river, as if she'd always known that it would call her back.

At the bottom of the lane she found the water high and fast after days of rain. The path was flooded right up to the wall, and the river level was high under the railway bridge. But Abren headed towards it without a qualm. Once she'd fought against that dark, old bridge, but she wouldn't fight again. It was where the river had first brought her – *and now it had brought her back again*.

Part Three
Dark River

Red

Most nights the town glowed a dull red. It went quiet at six when the workers went home, but was throbbing by ten. You could even hear it under the railway bridge. In between trains rumbling overhead, you could hear the club life around the station. Hear bass lines thumping and drums rattling, and people shouting to each other on their pub crawls round the town. And always they'd end up back here where they'd started, picking up taxis and buying late-night pizzas.

Tonight, however, the streets around the station stood silent and dark. All the clubs were closed, and there was little fun to be had out and about. No neon lights flashed cocktail-lounge signs or offered cheap beer. Even the station lights were out, the platforms standing silent with no trains running and no loudspeakers apologising for anything.

From his hidden world beneath the station, perched up on the girders, Phaze II looked out at the town. It might appear deserted, but he only had to draw back the darkness and there they all would be – the good people of Pengwern with their food and drink and stupid paper hats, their Christmas presents and crackers full of jokes, their tinsel trees and enough cash spent on just this one day to keep him going all year.

But that was scuds for you! Phaze II smiled grimly.

Stupid scuds – he hated the lot of them! He pulled his black coat round him, imagining the river rising until it was high enough to fill all their houses, never stopping until they'd been washed away. That'd show them! That'd cut them down to size!

Phaze II would have laughed out loud, but a crowd of boys came along. They entered the tunnel, shouting over the din of the swollen river. Water soaked their trousers and ran over their boots. But it didn't put them off. It ran against them in waves, but they splashed along the cobbles, breaking bottles and cheering to each other, never looking up to see a boy in the shadows watching everything they did.

Phaze II moved back out of sight, making sure to keep it that way. But he needn't have bothered. The boys were staggering, plainly drunk. They didn't know he was there. And neither, for that matter, did they know what danger they were in, larking about on a path whose edge, only inches away from them, lay under water.

But Phaze II knew. He watched their antics and waited for trouble. They were shouting at each other, fighting for the fun of it and chucking more bottles about. Then they fell quiet and Phaze II heard the hissing and rattling of spray cans, and caught a whiff of paint. He moved to get a better view. There were no streetlights underneath him, but it was still possible to make out the BC boys' special brand of Christmas greeting. It grew across the tunnel wall – a whole new layer of graffiti spelling out in shiny paint just where Jesus, Mary and the town of Pengwern could put their Christmas cheer.

Phaze II knew just how they felt, but it didn't make

him feel any better about them ruining his wall. He willed the boys to hurry up and finish. They had homes to go to, but this was all he'd got. He wanted it to himself, and he didn't want their ugly graffiti all over it. But as if they had no intention of going anywhere, the boys started yanking the doors off an electricity generator cage, ripping down grills for keeping out pigeons, and scrambling up the niches in the tunnel wall, trying to get up to the girders.

Phaze II turned away, feeling under threat. Before he could slip away into the darkness, however, a new figure appeared in the tunnel. It came wading along the path with its head down and shoulders hunched, obviously unaware that something nasty waited up ahead. There was nothing that Phaze II could do to warn it – not without giving himself away. He watched the figure approach the centre of the tunnel, where there were no lights and the boys were hanging off the wall. They saw the figure before it saw them – and jumped down in front of it.

Afterwards Phaze II blamed himself. It should have been possible for him to shout a warning without getting caught – a boy like him, who knew the bridge and all its secret getaways! But once the thing had started, there was nothing he could do. The figure looked up, and there they were – a crowd of BC boys bursting for trouble.

'Well, who do we have here?'

The figure realised that it was in trouble, and tried to back away. But it was already too late. Boys poured out of the shadows, crowding round and blocking off its retreat. Phaze II couldn't see what was happening, but he could hear them shouting and caught the words *witch* and *bitch* and *out, out, out.* Then the BC boys started pushing the figure about. It tried to break away from them – and suddenly Phaze II got a clear view.

It was the girl, again. The one who'd stared at her reflection in the market door, dressed up in that stolen sweater. The one he would have noticed anywhere, even if he hadn't dreamt about her, because there was something different about her. And the BC boys didn't like people who were different. They only liked people just like them. They were frightened of everybody else. *Even little girls.*

As Phaze II watched, they started laying into her. Obviously they thought that they could get away with it, here under the bridge on Christmas night with the river in full flood and nobody to see. They crowded round the girl, chanting at her and pointing their fingers as if her stumbling into them had made their day.

'Witch! Bitch! Out, out, out!'

Phaze II heard their spray-cans hissing and heard the girl's cry. Clouds of startled pigeons flew off into the night and the boys cheered. They sprayed again, and Phaze II caught the stink of paint. He reminded himself that the first golden rule was not to get involved. But the girl cried again, and he flushed red with shame. To think he'd seen this coming but hadn't done anything! And to think that he sat above it now – *and still he wasn't doing anything!*

The girl cried again. Phaze II didn't know what to do. A bottle smashed beneath him. And then the girl screamed.

For a moment silence fell.

Then, *'Bloody hell!'*

Suddenly, boys were disappearing in all directions – Border Commandos taking to the shadows, crying out in a panic as they melted into the night. No longer were they drunk, but stone-cold sober. Phaze II watched them running off as if they'd never stop. Try as he might, he couldn't see what had happened to the girl. She wasn't on the path any more. They hadn't taken her with them, and she hadn't run off down the tunnel.

The only place left was the river! Phaze II forced himself to look down, to where it swirled and crashed between the bridge's rows of iron legs. Perhaps the girl had fallen in by accident. Perhaps the BC boys hadn't meant to push her in. Perhaps she'd simply lost her footing and failed to see the edge. But she was down there, wasn't she? Phaze II couldn't see her, but he knew it in his bones.

And so did the boys.

'We're not to blame!' they shouted as they ran.

'We didn't do nothing!'

'It was all her own stupid fault!'

'Let's get out of here!'

Finally they were gone, and silence returned. Phaze II knew that tomorrow they would tell themselves that it hadn't even happened – that in some drunken stupor they'd imagined the whole thing. The fact that a body was found downriver would be just a coincidence. Nothing to do with them.

He stood upon the girders, red with anger as well as shame. Anger at the boys, and anger at himself. He should be jumping in the river and rescuing the girl. Even now every precious second could count. But he knew he wouldn't do it. He wasn't that sort of boy. Wasn't a hero or the sort to draw attention to himself. And he didn't trust the water, anyway. Never had done, for all that he lived on a bridge over a river.

Even when he saw the body, Phaze II knew he wouldn't do a thing. There it was right under him, waves breaking over it. And he knew he couldn't help. Not with the river in full flood. Not in the dark, with the water as cold as ice, and waves with jagged edges like hungry white teeth.

'I can't!' he shouted, peeling out of his coat.

'I won't!' he shouted, pulling off his boots.

'NEVER IN A MILLION YEARS!' he shouted – and he jumped.

Old Sabrina

Abren lay upon a concrete island. Something had got hold of her legs and something else was tugging in the opposite direction, with a grip under her shoulders. She didn't know where she was or how she had got there. She stared around her, trying to work it out. All around her were other islands in rows, massive iron pillars rising from them into a darkness which smelt cold and bitter. Waves crashed over them, swirling into whirlpools, then chasing each other off down-river.

'Where ...? What ...? *I don't understand!*'

Abren brushed a hand against her face, and found a swelling over one eye. She must have hit something, but couldn't remember what. Her hair was wet and stuck flat to her head. Her clothes were sodden and her blanket clung like wet ice to her shoulders. Suddenly a wave broke over her too, running down her and tugging at her legs.

Immediately the tugging under her shoulders doubled its efforts. *'You've got to move!'* a voice cried. 'You can't just lie there! You've got to help yourself! *I can't do this on my own!*'

Abren turned her head, feeling sick and giddy, and a boy came bobbing into her vision. He was as soaked as her, and shivering with the cold, holding on to her and trying to keep them both out of the water.

It was an impossible task. Abren felt his hands

under her shoulders again – and understood at last. This was the railway bridge, and she was on one of the concrete islands which held its iron legs. She had fallen into the river, forced over the edge by her confrontation with the BC boys, and now this other boy was rescuing her. Or trying to, if she'd only give him a chance!

'Don't just lie there! *You can do it!*' the boy cried.

Abren did her best, but it was a feeble effort. It would have been so much easier to let herself go. She kicked against the waves but they were a hundred times stronger than her. Tried to draw up her legs, but they seemed to weigh a ton. Hauled herself backwards, but struck cold iron.

She turned around and found herself pressed against some sort of cage which the boy was squeezing through – an easy task for someone as thin as him.

'*Come on!*' he yelled at Abren. 'You can't just stay there – the river's rising!'

Abren realised that the cage housed a metal service ladder. The boy started up it, and Abren would have been left behind if she hadn't hurried after him. She squeezed between iron bars and started climbing. Above her she could hear the boy coughing and shivering as if his freezing dip had done for him. She shivered in her wet clothes as if it had done for her too. By now her hands were white and she had lost all feeling. She couldn't get a proper grip, and had to bite her lip to force herself to keep alert. The higher she climbed, too, the less safe the ladder seemed. Some rungs were missing and others had lost their screws and hung loose.

Shaking with relief, Abren finally made it to the

solid safety of an iron-girder walkway. Here the boy was hauling himself into a big black coat and a pair of boots. Then, as if it was understood that Abren would follow him, he started along an iron walkway no more than half a metre wide, which stretched ahead of them without a handrail on either side.

'I can't do that,' Abren said.

The boy turned back. 'Of course you can!' he called. 'There's nothing to it. All you have to do is tell yourself that there's plenty of room – and just keep walking! It's easy once you've made a start. *Just don't look down.*'

'You must be joking!'

'I'm too cold to joke.'

The boy pulled his coat around him, bowed his head and coughed into his chest. Suddenly, Abren realised that she had seen him before. It had been in the market on Christmas Eve. He was the boy who'd stared at her and she'd stared back as if they'd known each other. A tall, thin boy in a black coat – and she'd seen him before that, too, going through the bins at the market.

Now, he returned along the girder, biting back his impatience and offering her a cold hand. She took it with reluctance. Slowly, they edged their way out over the river, Abren clinging to the boy's words about not looking down. When they reached the end, he didn't say 'well done'. He just let go of her hand and started up another service ladder and along a dizzying series of further girders until they reached the central core of black stone arches which formed the bridge's hidden spine.

Here they came to what seemed like a dead end.

There was no way forward on the girders, not that Abren could see. And there was no way back – at least not one that she could face.

'What do we do now?' she whispered, a dangerous wobble in her voice.

The boy looked at her coolly, and said, '*We jump.*'

'We *what*?' Abren replied.

The boy grinned tightly. 'There's a gap,' he said. 'Half a metre wide. Nothing much. You could always try to stretch across it if you want – but you'd probably lose your balance. *It's safer to jump.*'

Abren stared into the darkness. She couldn't see the gap and she couldn't see beyond it. And the boy could be lying. He could be playing games with her, just like those other boys. She felt herself panic, prickly and hot, forgot his advice and looked down at the river. There it was, black and full, running underneath her. But instead of making everything worse, it reassured her. The boy had rescued her from those dark waters, at a high cost to himself. He'd risked his life – and he wouldn't do that just to make her jump into oblivion! It didn't make sense.

So when he yelled, 'Jump!' Abren jumped. And maybe just for a split second she wished she hadn't, but then something hard rose up and smashed the soles of her feet. It was a floor! A good, solid, cold floor. Abren lay flat upon it as if she'd never get up again.

The boy struck a match. 'All right?' he said in a gruff voice which couldn't hide the fact that he was impressed.

Abren looked around her. She was in a low, stone chasm, its walls oozing stalactites of slimy white-lime mortar.

'Where are we?' she asked.

'We're underneath the railway,' the boy replied. 'Inside the arches, in the middle of the bridge. The station platforms are above us, and the river's underneath. But you'd never know it, would you? I mean, listen.'

Abren listened, but all she could hear was the boy shivering. His match went out and he lit another. Then he got up, pulling her after him.

'Stay close or you'll get lost,' he said.

He steered Abren through the darkness, lighting matches as they went. She stumbled over litter, and ducked under service pipes every time he warned her to mind her head. Her ears began to tune in to the silence, which wasn't as complete as she'd first thought. Distantly, she made out the mumble of an electricity generator, and closer to hand she heard the cooing pigeons in their roosts.

'And rats too,' the boy said. 'There'll be a few of them about as well.'

They reached the end of the chasm, and the boy said, 'Mind your head,' one last time. Abren stumbled up a short staircase and found herself before a metal-plated door, which was stuck ajar. The boy leant against it, shoved deftly with his shoulder and the door scraped open enough for them to slip through.

On the other side, Abren found herself in a space which she realised – with a shock – was actually lived in by someone. The boy switched on a single bulb hanging precariously from a swinging cable, and she saw a narrow room, full of what looked like rubbish, with a tea bar running down the length of it, complete with an old urn and stacks of china cups.

'British Rail cups, left over from the old days before polystyrene,' the boy said.

Abren stared around her. Behind the tea bar hung a rusty advertisement for Cadbury's chocolate, and next to it hung a mirror on a piece of string. The walls were covered with embossed brown paper, which was peeling. There were no windows – at least not that Abren could see. The floor was cluttered with black bin liners and cardboard boxes, and out of them spilled everything from old toasters and books and jumble-sale clothes.

The boy clambered over them to fiddle with a clump of dangling wires and switch on a bunch of plastic, icicle-shaped fairy lights. These hung over a splitting horse-hair mattress, illuminating its greasy cotton-ticking pillows with no covers, and grey stinking blankets, in a grim parody of a Santa's grotto. Maybe the boy thought that it looked Christmassy with lights, but Abren shivered.

As if he thought that she was cold, the boy reached into the nearest box and pulled out a choice of jumpers and thick pleated skirts, shell-suit trousers and tweedy jackets, all with the same fusty smell.

'You need to get out of those wet clothes,' he said. 'Take what you want.'

Abren took the clothes reluctantly. The boy's hands were like ice and he was turning blue, despite his thick coat. Even his lips were blue, and his eyes were dead.

'What about *you*?' she said.

Before the boy could answer, a bell rang out. His head shot up and he glanced at a door which Abren hadn't noticed before, at the end of the room, behind the tea bar.

'What's going on?' Abren said.

The boy didn't answer, just started rushing about. Abren watched as bread and butter appeared out of a box, followed by a half-opened tin of peaches, a cup of chocolate raisins and a mug of tea. The boy piled them all on to a tray made out of a cardboard lid and headed for the door.

'*What's going on?*' Abren repeated. 'What are you doing? Where are you going?'

The bell rang again, sharp and insistent. The boy pushed open the door and hurried through.

Abren followed, full of curiosity. On the other side she found another room which was as grand as the boy's was tawdry. Its floor was tiled and carpeted. Its gilt-framed mirror didn't hang on string. Its light wasn't a single bulb but a crystal chandelier. And beneath it stood not a tea urn with cheap cups but a fine piano with polished brasses and keys made of ivory.

Abren stared in amazement. Only later did she realise that the gilt-framed mirror was speckled with age, the ivory keys yellow and half the cut-glass droplets on the chandelier either cracked or missing. At the far end of the room stood an ornate marble fireplace, and in front of it sat a throne-like armchair, upholstered in red velvet and carved with leaves.

In the chair sat an old woman.

'I know I'm late. I'm sorry,' the boy said.

He hurried to the chair, put down the cardboard tray, removed the bell from the old woman's lap and replaced it with the bread and butter. The old woman picked at it with spidery little hands, and he danced attendance, throwing a fresh log on the fire to bring it back to life, then giving her the peaches, and then the raisins too, which she ate without leaving a single one.

All the while, she stared through the boy with flint-cold eyes. Stared as if he weren't there, and stared through Abren too.

'Do you want your cup of tea?' the boy asked when everything else was finished.

The old woman didn't answer, just turned away. The boy looked up and saw Abren watching. He blushed as if she'd caught him out.

'Meet Old Sabrina, queen of the river,' he said.

Millennium night

The boy lay covered up in blankets at one end of the mattress, and Abren lay at the other, curled up tight beneath a pile of old coats. The lights were out and in the darkness she could hear things scampering. She tried to sleep but couldn't. The day ran back through her mind, ending where it had started, with Santa's chocolates.

Now Dogpole Alley felt so far away, with its half-demolished turkey, its presents scattered everywhere and its glittering tree. Abren remembered Bentley playing 'her' tune on his new saxophone. She was sure he hadn't known what he was doing, but if it hadn't been for him, she wouldn't be lying here now, telling herself that she was where she should be, and there was nothing to be frightened of.

Not even Old Sabrina.

Abren pulled the coats around her and thought of the old woman asleep next door. She remembered the boy running at her beck and call. He'd shaken when he'd crossed the floor carrying that tray of tea things. And Abren didn't blame him. There was something weird about Old Sabrina. She hadn't thanked the boy for anything, or even smiled at him. Hadn't done a thing to help herself, just sat on that chair in her tightly buttoned, holey cardigan and long dusty skirt.

The boy had fetched her blankets and pillows and a footstool for her blotchy feet. He'd made her comfortable for the night – far more comfortable than he'd been himself in his wet clothes. But when he left the room, she still hadn't acknowledged him. It was as if she were a real queen and he her slave. When he'd said goodnight, she hadn't even answered him.

Abren shivered underneath the coats. Tried to forget the old woman and go to sleep. But how could she sleep when bursts of wheezy coughing kept firing off into the darkness, keeping even the rats awake.

'You ought to see a doctor with a cough like that!' she said at last.

The boy didn't answer, just coughed into his blankets until Abren couldn't stand it any more. She sat up, switched on the fairy lights, pulled back the blankets and found him fully dressed, boots and all, lying bathed in sweat. His eyes were bright, his face was white and he was shivering all over. This was no ordinary cough! He had caught a chill. And it was all because of her – because he'd jumped into the river to rescue her.

'You should have changed out of those wet clothes,' Abren said. '*I should have made you*. I could see how cold you were, but I didn't do a thing!'

She leapt off the mattress, overwhelmed with guilt, and went in search of the boy's grandmother, or godmother, or stepmother, or great-aunt, or whoever Old Sabrina might turn out to be. Never mind that she was weird! She was old, and would surely know how to nurse a sick boy.

Abren pushed open the door between the rooms, switched on the light and found Old Sabrina seated on the velvet chair exactly as they had left her, the only difference being that the fire had burned out. Abren padded forward until she was close enough to see the old woman's crumpled face, like a piece of thick old parchment, her tight mouth, sharp nose and fuzzy grey eyes. They weren't exactly dead, those eyes, but they stared blankly, like windows in a house which nobody lived in any more.

'Excuse me,' Abren said, 'but the boy's ill. I don't know what to do. I think he needs a doctor.'

The eyes didn't move. Old Sabrina wasn't asleep, but it was as if she hadn't heard. Abren tried again, standing right in front of her, and then again, shouting in her face. But it made no difference. Abren could stay here all night if she wanted, but the eyes would never change. They'd never look at her. Never take any notice.

Abren left the room. Perhaps the old woman was crazy. Perhaps that was what it was. Back next door, she found the boy on his feet, staggering about as if her shouting, though it hadn't stirred Old Sabrina, had certainly stirred him. A kettle had been plugged in, and he was rummaging through boxes containing magazines, rat poison, bath oil, soap, computer games and mounds of clothes, looking for medicine. This he found at last in a zip-up bag containing everything from aspirins to plasters and honey linctus syrup, which was a wonder cure that 'did for everything', according to the boy. He glugged some down, despite the warning on the bottle about proper measurements, dissolved a lemon cold-cure in some water from the kettle and returned to bed.

Abren returned too, but only after making sure that the door was tightly shut between her and Old Sabrina. Then exhaustion overwhelmed her and she fell asleep. It happened very quickly. One minute she was drifting off, her thoughts returning to Dogpole Alley, and the next minute she was waking up, still thinking of it but a whole night had gone by.

Abren lay in the darkness imagining her empty bedroom, with Christmas-stocking paper strewn about and nobody around to pull back the curtains. She wondered if Bentley would be awake yet. And Fee and Mena. Had they been up all night, searching for her? Been to the police and told them all about her? Taken down the decorations, Christmas forgotten as if they knew that she wouldn't ever come back?

For the next few days, the boy was sick. Abren wanted to look after him, but he made her go and look after Old Sabrina. Her need was greater, he insisted. She couldn't even hobble to the toilet without help.

Abren didn't want to help the old woman, but with the boy threatening to drag himself off his sickbed and do it instead, she had little choice. In the mornings, she made up a fire. Then she fed Old Sabrina out of what the boy called the 'Best-by-End-of Chest' – a rat-proof metal box with a tight lid, into which he put the food he'd either bought with cash or scrounged out of bins. Then she bathed the old woman's face and hands and blotchy feet. Then she tidied up her bird's nest of white hair – though why she bothered she didn't know, because it was always messy minutes later.

Then she stayed close by, dancing attendance should Old Sabrina need to be taken to the rusty-chained toilet or require more fuel on the fire. She brought food when the bell rang, and even chased spiders out of the old woman's lap when they started making webs as if she were a dead object, not a person. And she tried to talk to the old woman.

In this last effort, Abren's time was wasted more than in any other. Old Sabrina obviously didn't want any conversation. She wouldn't look at Abren, let alone answer any of her questions about who she was, how long she'd been here, how she'd found this limbo-land of old abandoned waiting rooms, and where she'd come from in the first place. She never asked for anything except by using the bell, and at the end of each day, when Abren had prepared her for the night and was heading off through the door, she didn't thank her for anything.

'How do you stand her?' Abren asked one night, flopping down on her end of the mattress.

'I keep my head down and I don't think. Don't ask questions – just get on with it,' the boy said.

The next morning, to Abren's relief, the boy was better. He got up looking like a new boy, washed himself in a kettle full of water and introduced himself by the unlikely name of Phaze II. His cough hadn't cleared up, but he was in good spirits. He ate a quick breakfast and went to 'do' Old Sabrina.

She didn't ask if he was better, but he didn't seem to mind. He washed her like a baby – face, neck, arms, hands, feet – struggled with her tangled hair, brushed a mixture of crumbs and dust out of her lap and found a new cardigan, which he buttoned over the previous ones to keep her warm. Finally, he produced a pair of socks which he pulled over her blotchy-looking, red-and-blue feet.

'Keep them on,' he said. 'Don't mess around and pull them off. I'm going out for food. You'll be all right, won't you? I'll see you later.'

Later meant that night. It was a long day for Abren without the sound of his coughing, which she had grown strangely attached to. But finally he came back, scrambling through a boarded-up window which Abren hadn't even known was there, bringing mackerel, olives and chocolates with him. They had all passed their sell-by date and the chocolates had acquired a speckled bloom. But Abren scoffed down everything she was given – and was promptly sick.

Phaze II took her out on the girders to get some fresh air. He said this often happened, eating old food past its prime.

'But your stomach'll get used to it, just like mine.'

The two of them sat on the girders, swinging their legs high above the river. Abren pulled her little blanket around her. It was the first time she'd been out since Christmas night and she was astonished at how cold it was after the fusty warmth of the waiting rooms. Overwhelmed, too, by the freshness of the air and the brightness of the stars. It was a beautiful night.

Phaze II said that it was a special night – New Year's Eve when everybody went out partying. And not just any New Year's Eve, but the one the scuds called 'the Millennium'.

Abren didn't know what he was talking about, and Phaze II looked at her as if she'd landed from another planet.

'Where have you been?' he asked. 'Everybody's on about it. A once-in-a-thousand-years experience! The moving-on of time from one age to another! The biggest global party since the Big Bang!'

Abren felt sick again. She leant over the girder and heaved into the river. Afterwards she felt weak enough to drop, and Phaze II had to hold on to her.

'That'll be the last of it,' he said, with an air of expertise. 'You've emptied out your stomach. You'll be all right now.'

Abren leant against him – a tall gangling boy in a flapping coat, who was the nearest she had to a friend. Suddenly all the questions came out again. The ones she'd asked Old Sabrina, and a few new ones too.

'Why Phaze II?' she asked. 'What sort of name is that? Did Old Sabrina give it to you? Is she your grandmother? And if not, who *is* she? What's she doing here? How did you ever find this place? And how did she?'

Out it poured in an endless stream. In the end Phaze II held up his hands, crying for mercy. He couldn't possibly answer all those questions, he said, but he could tell her that Old Sabrina wasn't his grandmother, and that she hadn't given him his name.

'But she *did* give me a home,' he said. 'And I'll never forget her for it. She mightn't have much else to give, but in the empty kingdom of the railway bridge she's made me her crown prince!'

He laughed and, just for a moment, a faraway expression appeared on his face as if there was a story here, but he wasn't telling it. Abren shivered. She wanted to ask so much more, but suddenly the town erupted. Cheers and shouts burst out across the night, starting in the Quarry Park and quickly spreading along the old town walls. What was going on? A cannon thundered in the castle garden and the town's bells started ringing. Fireworks shot into the sky in golden chrysanthemums, red star sprays, fountains of phutting violet and rainbow rockets which whooshed through the dark. Klaxons whirred, sirens wailed and whistles shrieked.

Phaze II produced a can of lager from his black coat. He ripped it open, took a swig and offered some to Abren.

'This is it!' he said. 'Twelve midnight! The twenty-first century arrives – and will it be different from all the other ones? Will it really? What do *you* think?'

Abren didn't answer. She didn't know what he was on about. The cheers grew louder, and the town's bells rang on and on. She took a small sip of lager, then a bigger one. The world began to whirl around her in a mass of yet more fireworks and laser lights. The air was alive with cheers and chimes, the sky so bright that she imagined it never turning dark again. Even the river was brilliant with light – a golden river reflecting all those fireworks as it disappeared beneath the railway bridge, out of sight.

Abren tried to hold herself upright. The whirling world was making her giddy. She'd stop that river if she could. Stop it flowing and keep the moment steady. Freeze the fireworks in the sky. Stop the midnight clock. Make the celebration calm down. Stop time moving on and make it stand still.

'This could be a dream,' Phaze II said. 'Not one that wakes you in a panic, but one that makes you never want to wake at all. A perfect dream, which you want to keep for ever. What do you think?'

'I think you got it wrong about my stomach being empty!' Abren said, leaning forward to be sick.

Remembering

Time moved on, flowing like the river out of sight. The days passed like a dream. Not Phaze II's perfect dream, but one that was impossible to keep for ever. Occasionally the days brought wonders with them – snow on rooftops and frost on the river; pale clouds of mist and swans floating between foamy waters like dancers in a silent ballet. But mostly the days were cold and dull. Clouds blew in from Plynlimon Mountain in mid-Wales, where Phaze II said that the river began. Rain fell remorselessly and the river water, which had been so golden on Millennium Night, became a silty brown sludge. No sun offered brightness to its journey and the sky was as grey as the landscape it presided over.

On these days Abren would curl up tight, hibernating on the camp bed which Phaze II had found for her on a rubbish tip. Trains would rumble by, shaking everything, but she had become so used to them that she didn't notice. Rats would scamper by, and pigeons coo in their roosts. But Abren didn't notice anything. She had left Dogpole Alley on a brave adventure, but now she didn't feel so brave.

It was as if the darkness had got her in its grip. When Phaze II went to town, she wouldn't go with him. When he asked her to keep Old Sabrina company, she wouldn't even do that any more, but hid out on the girders. The old woman frightened her with her blank, unseeing eyes. The girders were far less scary, for all their dizzying height.

Abren would sit out on them, watching people going by. They'd come into the tunnel, their heads down. *Scuds*, Phaze II called them. Stupid Cruddy Ugly Dumb people, living in Stupid Cruddy Ugly Dumb houses and working at Stupid Cruddy Ugly Dumb jobs, never looking up, always looking down, always in a hurry somewhere, busy and important. Abren watched them bustling on their way, people from another world who couldn't see her sitting up above them. It was as if the railway bridge wrapped itself around her like an invisible cloak.

The days continued to pass in a dream, and winter turned to spring without Abren noticing. One Friday night she sat up late listening to an outdoor concert in the Quarry Park. A throng of music fans roared themselves hoarse, and Abren watched them noisily dispersing across the English Bridge. Finally the park's floodlights went out and everything fell quiet.

For the first time Abren realised that it was a lovely night. She looked upriver to the English Bridge where a little mist lingered and stars hung over the rim of the mist. The air wasn't clammy, as it had been for weeks. It didn't soak into her bones, but was light and fragrant.

Spring was on the way and Abren noticed at last. As if to prove the point, a blackbird started singing. The middle of the night, yet it trilled and crooned as if it were day!

Abren thrilled to the sound of sunshine in the blackbird's song. It was singing for her alone, with nobody else to enjoy it.

Or so Abren thought – until the saxophone joined in! It was Bentley's saxophone, of course. She didn't need to see him to recognise his unmistakable style. Abren listened as his notes rose among the girders, catching their own echo and playing back with it. No one but Bentley could do that, picking up the sounds around him, whether blackbirds or the river, and making something of them.

Abren crept along the girders until she could see him standing in the cobbled tunnel under her. His face looked up, but his eyes were closed. Abren hadn't thought about him for weeks, and now here he was. She waited for him to move on to 'her' tune. The one that sang to her with its strange enchantment. And he surely would. He'd play 'her' tune, and she would wake up from her winter dreaming. It would make her strong again, and brave enough to shake off this dark limbo-land and move on.

Abren held her breath and waited. Beneath her Bentley played until his lungs and lips and fingers had been blown to pieces. And she listened until the last note faded. But he didn't play 'her' tune. She watched him pack away the saxophone, toss its case over his shoulder, then start off along the tunnel, never knowing the disappointment he left behind.

Abren willed him to return, but he trudged down the river path and never once turned back. She watched him disappearing. Phaze II tried to make her come in, but she barked out that she wanted to be alone. She remained like that for most of the night, still willing Bentley to come back, but he never did.

In the end she fell asleep, with only the narrow ledge between her and the river. It was a miracle that she didn't fall in. She awoke in the morning to sunrise over the English Bridge. But she didn't notice it. Spring was in the air, and the blackbird was singing again, but it didn't raise her spirits.

Abren sat up on the bridge, feeling strangely empty, as if a chance had come her way but then been snatched back. When Phaze II came high-wiring along the girders to ask if she was all right, she didn't even answer. He carried on to town as if he couldn't care less whether she wanted to talk to him, and had better things to do with his time, anyway.

When he had gone, Abren went back inside, looking for breakfast after a night out in the cold. But no food remained in the Best-by-End-of Chest, only a mess of rotting leftovers which even Phaze II's hardened stomach obviously hadn't been able to take. Abren searched the entire room, rummaging among Phaze II's boxes and bin bags, and beneath the long counter of the tea bar, but finding only china plates with mould growing over them. A pall of dust covered everything – a lurid, grubby sheen lit by plastic icicles.

Abren looked at it all, and suddenly she hated it. Hated the mess, and the manky smell which came from bodies living without proper ventilation. Hated Old Sabrina's wretched bell which had started ringing as if she'd heard someone moving about. And, worst of all, she hated herself.

'What's the matter with me? Am I crazy? I might have had to stay when Phaze II was sick, but I don't have to stay now! What a dump! I mean, *look at it!*'

Old Sabrina rang again. Abren went through to find that the fire had gone out and a plate of food had fallen off the old woman's lap. It was obvious what

Abren was supposed to do, but she strode down the room to Phaze II's boarded-up window. She was off, she told herself, never to return! Let Old Sabrina freeze before the ashes of her fire! Let her food rot on the plate, if she wouldn't pick it up for herself!

Leaving the bell ringing, Abren squeezed out of the window on to a rusty, disused railway track. Weeds grew between the sleepers, and litter lay everywhere. A stony bank rose in front of Abren, and along the top of it stood a row of advertising hoardings upon which massive toucans, torn and ragged, advertised a drink called Guinness. Beyond the hoardings stood an old station platform, abandoned in favour of a modern station across the tracks.

Abren climbed the stony bank, squeezed between the hoardings and jumped on to the platform. Here she discovered that it spanned the river, forming one side of the railway bridge. She hurried away, hoping that nobody would notice her. At the end of the platform she found an iron gate. She slipped through it, passing a sign which read RAIL PERSONNEL ONLY, and found a footpath on the other side, cutting down between the station and the castle. Following it, she found herself in town.

Here the bustle came as a shock after weeks hidden in the darkness. People pushed around Abren as if she were in the way. Everybody seemed in a hurry except for her. What was she doing here? She didn't know. Where was she going? She didn't have a clue.

She reached the high town cross, and the sun shone all the way down Pride Hill. Abren looked at daffodils in tubs and leaves bursting on the trees. Blackbirds sang and sparrows chirruped between rooftops. This wasn't the town Abren had left on Christmas night. It was a new town, and a new day. And suddenly it was a new adventure too. Never mind that Abren didn't know where she was going or what would happen next! She started down the hill, determined to make the most of things – and starting off by finding a ten-pound note lying in the gutter.

A ten-pound note! Abren snatched it up, and bought herself a bowl of soup and three enormous pieces of chocolate cake, one after another. Then, upon a whim, she bought a postcard for Bentley – a typical tourist view of the river. She scribbled a message on the back, saying that she was alive, safe and well, and there was nothing for him to worry about. As an afterthought, she said how much she'd enjoyed his playing under the bridge, and she finished off by signing her name.

Then she stuck the postcard in the Bytheways' letter box, remembering that other card she'd sent to keep Mena happy – the blank card with no signature or message.

At least I've got someone to send it to this time, she thought. And I've got something to say and a name to sign!

She hurried down Dogpole Alley, feeling as cheerful as she'd done for weeks, and emerged into Old St Chad's Square to find it full of yet more daffodils. The old church was bright, the crows on its walls were preening their feathers in the sunshine and even St Chad's crypt had caught a bit of sunlight.

Abren started up the grassy mound, in the best of spirits. Birds swooped and sang among the trees, waiting for the Chadman to start feeding them. It was his time, obviously. He came up the mound from the other side, carrying plastic bags which bulged with sandwiches and seed, whistling the birds down through his long teeth.

Abren watched them spiralling down, undeterred by his ragged clothes, matted hair and beard, and feet bursting out of old boots. Which of Mena's stories about him had been right? Abren wondered. Was he a merchant banker fallen on hard times? A teacher caught up in a scandal? A baby born without blood getting to his brain? The Chadman drew close, but he didn't see Abren. All he had eyes for were his friends, the birds.

Or so it seemed until a mother and her toddler daughter came over the mound towards him. The toddler ran up to him and started chattering as if they were old friends. She smiled at him and he smiled back, filling her cupped hands with birdseed. The mother smiled too, as if this meeting were a perfectly normal occurrence.

She came and joined them, taking birdseed too, and it was a nice moment between the three of them. A pink-breasted chaffinch came and sat on the little girl's hands. It pecked the seed, and they all beamed. The mother nodded to the Chadman as if to say thank you, and if he hadn't been in rags, and she so clean and tidy, they could have been a proper little family.

Phaze II would have sneered at them for being scuds. But Abren smiled along with them. It was a nice moment for her, too. But then a second woman appeared, spoiling everything. She came pounding up the mound from the iron-gated houses at the far side of the square, heading for the child and shouting something.

Abren watched her coming, paralysed by sudden fear. She couldn't make out what the woman was shouting, but suddenly she couldn't breathe properly, couldn't think straight or speak. Her sense of dread was overwhelming. She wanted to shout, 'Go quickly, while you can! Get out of here! *Flee ...*'

But all she could do was flee herself!

Leaving the child crying, the mother powerless to stop the shouting woman, and the Chadman staring blankly as if none of this were happening, Abren tore out of the square. She didn't want to see what took place next. She didn't dare. It was as if some awful thing had happened here. *And she ran in terror of remembering.*

Football fever

Abren ran and hid and ran again for half the day, tearing round the town as if looking for a way out. She didn't know what had got into her, but she felt as if she were being stalked. Once she saw Phaze II, but she darted down an alley and hid behind a rubbish bin until he'd gone. Then she started running again.

If only she could leave the town – cross the river and leave the horseshoe loop behind – perhaps then she would be safe. She headed for the Welsh Bridge, but everybody seemed to be staring at her strangely, and she turned back. Something had been triggered in her memory, but she didn't know what it was. She saw Phaze II again – a face in a busy crowd – and turned away in a panic.

It was ridiculous, of course. Phaze II was her friend, who had come along the girders to ask if she was all right. But suddenly Abren felt as if she couldn't trust even him. She hurried across town, heading for the English Bridge and getting caught up in a football crowd. With relief, she found herself surrounded by good-humoured supporters, nothing more threatening on their minds than beating the away team. Men and women, boys and girls, they all merged together into a sea of blue-and-white. And with her head down, Abren tagged along with them, hoping that she'd blend in.

The bridge approached and she moved towards it,

her heart thundering. Town supporters jostled her on either side, and she started on to the bridge, expecting a hand to tap her on the shoulder and drag her back. But she reached the end of the bridge, and three roads stretched ahead of her, signposted to *'Birmingham'*, *'Historic Ironbridge – Birthplace of the Industrial Revolution'* and *'London'*. Abren didn't know where any of these places were, but the river lay behind her, and so did Pengwern.

Suddenly she felt free. She headed for the nearest road, full of expectation. But before she could get more than a couple of steps, a crowd of away supporters came surging off a coach right in front of her. They were impossible to withstand – a tight wedge of men and boys who swept her along with them. No amount of crying to be let go made any difference. They were so preoccupied with getting to the match on time that they didn't notice Abren. Out of the corner of her eye, she saw her road disappear, and then the other two as well. Then she was carried into the ground, through the turnstiles, crushed up tight, and on to the stands.

Here a new sight greeted her. Not the football pitch, ready for the game with crowds around it waiting for the whistle, but the town viewed from the far side of the river. Abren stared at it – a patchwork of old stone mansions, towers and spires and modern office buildings. She saw the castle on the skyline, saw the roof of the new shopping mall, saw the old infirmary and the houses and flats nestled into the old town walls. Saw treetops swaying in a light spring breeze, and crows circling over them.

Then a whistle blew and the game began. On every

side of Abren, men and boys started yelling words of wisdom. The ball ran down the pitch and their advice ran after it. And not just theirs; whole families of mothers, fathers, brothers, sisters, grannies and grandpas were yelling at the two teams not to let them down.

Abren chose the moment to slip away. She trod round toes as best she could, tried not to knock into anybody's ribs or dislodge anybody's drink. She tried not to spoil anybody's view. But for all her efforts she ended up only a few feet down the stand. She started again, heading off in another direction. But this proved no more successful. Finally, fed up with being careful, she charged like a bull – straight into Phaze II.

'What are you doing here?'

'What are *you* doing here?'

'Why are you following me?'

'Who says I'm following you?'

'Don't play with me – I know you are.'

'Well, what if I am? You've been running round the town like a mad thing. Something's obviously wrong.'

'I don't know what you mean.'

'*Oh, yes, you do.*'

Abren tried to get away, but before she could something happened on the pitch. The town fans cheered, and the away fans started shaking their fists. They shouted vile things, and Abren found herself surrounded by men and boys with angry-looking, twisted faces.

She started pushing her way between them, startled by their voices and the violence in their faces. Phaze II chased after her, refusing to be left behind. Every time she turned around, there he was. She reached the end of the stand, and the away team scored a goal, setting their away fans crowing this time, and the town supporters crying foul.

Obviously, this was no ordinary match, but a battle between mortal enemies! Abren tried all the harder to get away. The voices were turning nasty.

'Bloody Welsh!' they cried. 'Kill the scrubbers! Break their legs! Die, die, die! Out, out, out!'

It sounded like an action replay of the BC boys' graffiti. And indeed it was! Abren looked around her and realised that for all her trying to get out of trouble, she had surrounded herself with Border Commandos! She tried to hide her face from them, but wasn't quick enough. The boys saw her – the selfsame boys who'd chased her and sprayed paint at her and driven her into the river. Now they stared at her again *and recognised who she was.*

For a terrible moment, Abren expected them to take up where they'd left off. But then – as if they'd seen a ghost, back to haunt them from the grave – the boys turned white, every single one of them.

'No! It can't be ...! *Bloody hell!*'

Suddenly, there was a stampede in the stands – BC boys disappearing in all directions, crushing everything that got in their way. Abren managed to jump aside, but Phaze II wasn't quick enough. They knocked him to the ground and the last thing Abren saw was his black coat as they pounded over him.

'It's her!'

'*That girl!*'

'It can't be!'

'*It is!*'

No longer could Abren see Phaze II. She called for

help, but no one came. She tried to reach the place where he had fallen, but couldn't find him. She dived beneath the crowd, and the world down there was made of boots. They all looked the same, and all felt as cold and hard as steel. But Abren struggled between them. She had to find Phaze II. She alone was to blame for whatever he was going through.

In the end it was Phaze II's cough that led Abren to him. His unmistakable cough! She heard it on the ground somewhere, and pushed her way towards it until there he was, slumped in a corner against a corrugated fence. A trickle of blood was coming out of his ear, his nose was swollen and one eye was half-closed. But he still managed to grin at Abren when she reached him.

'Glad you found me,' he said – and suddenly he was Abren's friend again, not someone to run away from. 'Let's get out of here.'

Abren followed as he hauled himself to his feet and led her along the back of the corrugated fence, weaving behind BC boys, Day-Glo stewards who had come at last to see what was going on, away fans who'd got caught up in something beyond their understanding, and police. Finally they reached a gap at the bottom of the fence. Phaze II dragged Abren through on hands and knees.

On the other side she found herself on a tree-lined earth path between the river and the railway bridge. A tunnel ran through the bridge, exactly matching the tunnel on the town shore, except that it wasn't cobbled and had no light. Abren looked into it, and suddenly felt as if she'd come home. She didn't want to run away to London. Didn't know why she'd ever left.

She headed for the bridge, and Phaze II followed her, although his eye was weeping and he would have done better to find himself a doctor. It was as if their fortunes were bound together. They reached the tunnel and started climbing up its inside wall, inching from brick to brick and niche to niche until they reached the girders. Here the darkness of the bridge wrapped itself around them, hiding them from BC boys and Day-Glo stewards and anything else that might come after them.

Phaze II grinned at Abren and his face said *home again*. He jumped the jump and she did too. Then the two of them felt their way through the dark chasm, stumbled up the flight of steps and forced their way through the metal door. And even when they switched on the light to reveal the narrow tea-bar room, just as dismal as when Abren had left it, they still felt as if they'd come home.

Abren walked down the room. She didn't mind the mess of smelly leftovers, or the mould, or the dust settled over everything. Didn't mind the manky smell which came from bodies living without proper ventilation. Didn't even mind Old Sabrina next door.

The bell was silent, as if Old Sabrina had worn herself out with ringing. Abren went to check that everything was all right, and found the room exactly as she'd left it. The mirror, the piano, the cut-glass chandelier, the marble fireplace. Even Old Sabrina's chair was just as she had left it.

The only difference was the old woman herself. *She wasn't there.*

'Old Sabrina's gone!' Abren called.

'She can't be,' Phaze II called back. 'She's always there. *Of course she hasn't gone!*'

He came running, but Abren was right. He checked between the bin bags in his room, in case Old Sabrina had had a fall. Checked the toilet. Squeezed between the boards and checked the bit of rusty railway track outside. Checked the old abandoned platform, and then returned to check his room again, turning everything over and looking increasingly worried.

Finally, he returned to Old Sabrina's room as if expecting her to have returned and the whole thing to have been some crazy joke. Not that Old Sabrina ever made jokes.

'She must be here!' he said.

Abren didn't answer. She was too busy blaming herself, yet again. She was the one, after all, who'd left the poor old woman ringing her bell. Phaze II said he'd go and double-check the toilet, and she said she'd go back down the chasm, taking a torch with her to get in all the corners. Her mind was full of rivers running underneath them, and girders without handrails, and places where the only way forward was to jump. She could imagine Old Sabrina stumbling forward on her swollen feet, and missing her step. Imagine her being swept away – *and Abren knew how that felt, didn't she?*

She was halfway to the door, when it juddered open. But it wasn't Old Sabrina who came through, to set her mind at rest. It was a uniformed policeman. He took one look at Abren.

'*Seems like we've found what we're looking for,*' he said.

Part Four
River Secrets

Compass House

It was the postcard that had done it – Abren's scribbled note to Bentley which praised his playing under the railway bridge. Mena read it and insisted on going to the police as she'd promised them she would when she'd reported Abren missing at Christmas. Bentley tried to make her come with him and search the bridge instead. But she wouldn't listen, and now it seemed that a nest of homeless children had been found hiding in the spaces above the girders. Everyone was talking about it all around the town. The children had been carted off to the police station and Mena was refusing to go and identify one of them as Abren.

She was also refusing – with absolute determination – to have 'that child' back until her real family were found. She wouldn't even have her back for a single meal, brought home by Fee who had gone to make the identification instead. She didn't want any further part in 'that child's' story, she said.

Fee reasoned that it made sense for them to take her back, at least for now. Bentley pleaded too, but Mena wouldn't have it. Abren was trouble, she said. You could see it in her eyes. See something odd about her. Something wild and strange and unpredictable. It had been a mistake ever getting involved.

'That child was born to trouble, you mark my words,' she said.

So Abren ended up with yet another set of strangers

entering her life, in yet another home that wasn't her own. This time it was on the old town walls, in the Morgans' place – Compass House. She stood outside it, on the narrow strip of pavement between wall and road. In front of her rose a narrow tower which looked more like a prison than anything else. Beside her stood a social worker, the policeman who had found her in the first place, and Phaze II. He hadn't spoken since they'd left the bridge, but from his glares Abren guessed he blamed her for everything.

The policeman banged on the knocker for the second time, and Phaze II shuffled restlessly as if he knew this was his last chance to get away. Abren heard feet dragging on the other side of the heavily studded front door, and a jangling sound which could have been a gaoler with a bunch of keys. She wondered what they were in for.

'All right, all right, I hear you,' a voice called, and the door creaked open to reveal not the dingy horror which Abren had expected, but a bright white hall.

Abren beamed, weak with relief, and the woman standing at the door beamed back. She was tall, with jangling bracelets instead of gaoler's keys, waist-long, yellow, curling hair and a bright pink-lipstick smile slapped across her face like a flyer on a billboard – there for all the world to read and impossible to shift.

She stepped aside to let them in. 'We've been expecting you. *Come in!* You're just in time for supper. I'm Mrs Morgan. Mrs Penny Morgan, but you must call me Pen.'

Phaze II scowled as if the only name that he would ever call her started with an S for scud. But Abren stepped over the threshold, wondering what fairyland she'd found behind this little tower with its studded door. Yet again, it seemed that appearances had proved deceptive. Or, as Fee had once said, you should never judge a book by its cover!

She followed Pen down the scrubbed white hall, which smelt of wood polish and was full of paintings, fish in cases, a long willow basket and an old cutlass hanging on the wall. At the end of the hall, they descended a flight of steps to a kitchen built out over the back of the house. Here all the clutter of a busy life was spread around a bright red stove. Seedlings grew in trays, under sheets of glass. A pile of vegetable peelings sat on a wooden chopping board. Glasses of red wine waited, half drunk, to be finished off. A basket of duck-blue eggs sat in bowl on the window ledge.

Phaze II stood in the doorway, staring at it all as if nothing could impress him. But Abren was enthralled. Never in her wildest dreams had she expected her day to end like this! She stared at the supper which the woman, Pen, lifted out of the stove, shutting the oven door behind her with the back of her heel. Whatever was in that cooking pot smelt wonderful. Abren fondly imagined it containing stew with dumplings, followed by a pudding drenched in chocolate sauce.

'Sit down,' Pen said. 'Eat while it's hot. Sir Henry isn't in yet. I've called and called. But that's him for you! Make a start without him.'

Abren sat down, wondering what sort of man was called *Sir Henry* by his own wife. She tried to catch Phaze II's eye but he looked away, refusing to turn back even when Pen served food on to his plate. She offered helpings to the social worker and the policeman too, but they said that they had to leave.

Pen went to see them out. She was gone a while and returned alone. Abren's plate had been scraped clean, but Phaze II's plate hadn't been touched.

'Oh, dear, you don't like chicken curry! Can I get you something else?'

'The boy will eat when he wants. Don't fuss. Leave him alone.'

At the sound of a new voice, Abren looked up to see a skinny black man standing at the back door. He was as tall as Pen, but stretched out like a taut wire. His cheekbones were high, and his eyes were full of something Abren couldn't quite identify, but she soon found out was laughter. His hair was salt-and-pepper grey, and he wore an old sailor's jersey. A clay pipe stuck out of his mouth, and a thin twist of something that smelt quite unlike tobacco came coiling out of it.

'Meet Mr Morgan,' Pen said. 'You can call him Henry if you want to, but hardly anybody does. *Sir Henry*'s what most people know him as. After his famous ancestor, you understand, the chief of all the buccaneers, who made his fortune in the Caribbean plundering the Spanish Main. Not that we've seen much of his famous fortune though – apart from the old blunt cutlass hanging in the hall.'

Sir Henry laughed at her, and she beamed round, embracing all of them with her mile-wide smile. Abren thought that she could never call the man Sir Henry. It was a silly name. She looked at Phaze II to see what he thought.

'What that boy needs isn't food, anyway. It's his bed,' Sir Henry said.

He was right. Phaze II was visibly wilting. His

bruises had come out like swollen prunes soaked in tea. His shoulders were sagging. His good eye was closing and Abren guessed that his other one – examined by a doctor at the police station, and covered in an enormous bandage – was now tightly shut. It had been an unexpected end to what had started as an ordinary day. And now he was exhausted.

They both were. One look at Abren too, and Pen took them upstairs to their beds. Abren's was a single room with a big, squashy bed and not much space for anything else. A sliding glass door opened out on a balcony. A paper lantern hung from the ceiling and long strips of red paper dangled over the bed. These were decorated with painted beads and feathers, and golden lettering which – according to Pen – wished all who slept beneath them sweet dreams.

Phaze II's room was bigger and contained sweet-dream banners too. It also contained bunk beds, an enormous hammock strung between beams, a model of one of Sir Henry Morgan's many warships and a glass case full of books. The floor was made of golden boards which gave off a lovely, woody, polished smell. And behind another sliding door stood a second balcony.

'I hope you like it,' Pen said.

Phaze II stared in silence. Abren could see that Pen was proud of the room. But as far as he was concerned, it was just a stupid scud's room. Nothing special.

'I'll leave you to get settled in,' Pen said. 'The bathroom's next door. There are towels on the bath, and pyjamas warming in the airing cupboard if you want them. Oh, and there's ointment in the medicine cabinet if you need it for that face of yours.'

She slipped away, no questions asked about how Phaze II had got that face of his with its big, ripe bruises. He pulled down all the sweet-dream banners, and Abren went to investigate the bathroom. She found it a blue-tiled dream of thick pile carpets, snowy enamel basins and shining chrome taps. Phaze II came in after her, still not a word said between them. He sat on the toilet with the lid down while Abren found the ointment, tilted him into the light and attended to his face. She started with his nose, applying the ointment generously, and finishing up covering most of his skin.

'I'm sorry,' she whispered every time that Phaze II winced.

Phaze II didn't answer, and Abren felt to blame for everything. Not just the bruises and all that trouble with the BC boys. But that stupid postcard, too, announcing to the world where she was hiding. And Mena's hurt feelings. And Fee's face when he'd told her that she couldn't go back home with him. And Old Sabrina's disappearance.

Everything was Abren's fault.

You'd think that I was cursed. Everything I touch turns sour, Abren thought. Everyone I come across ends up being hurt. And now it'll happen to these people too – Pen and Sir Henry. I've entered their lives and they'll wish I hadn't! Something terrible will happen to them, and it will all be my fault.

Phaze II got up, still without a word, and went to bed. Abren took a bath, marvelling at the filthy state of the water when she got out. Then she went to bed

106

as well, thinking that sleep would come easily. But it turned out to be impossible, for all Pen's banners wishing sweet dreams. Maybe it was the bed, its mattress as soft as marshmallow after nights spent sleeping on a camp bed. Or maybe it was a sense of foreboding about what tomorrow might bring.

Abren lay rigid in the bed. Down the landing she could hear Pen and Sir Henry laughing and talking to each other until long after their bedroom light had gone out. Their voices made Abren feel lonely. She missed Phaze II. Not just talking to him in the darkness, but the sound of his breathing as well, and that hacking cough of his and the way he sometimes shouted in his sleep.

In the end she got up and went to his door. She half expected to find that he had run away, but he lay stretched out on the bottom bunk, with not a muscle moving. Abren thought of waking him, but she didn't dare. Phaze II was a mystery. Even after all this time she still never knew how he would react to things.

So she went back to her room instead, and stood out on the balcony. The night was clear and mild, stars in the sky but the moon nowhere to be seen. House lights were out all over town and everything was quiet. Abren leant against the railing, looking down a steeply terraced garden. At the bottom she could see something dark moving away between the trees. It was the river, of course. Always the river in this town – there was no getting away from it.

Abren watched it flowing past a long jetty with a boat shed built behind it, half screened by trees. Someone had left a light on inside the shed and she could see a pile of wooden planks stacked on shelves.

See another basket, too, like the willow one hanging in the hall, and a row of paint tins.

Suddenly, Abren felt as if she could sleep at last. She didn't care that she and Phaze II hadn't made up. Didn't care what had happened to Old Sabrina. Didn't care that she'd spent half the day running round the town in a state of terror, chased by nothing more substantial than a half-memory. She didn't even care what tomorrow would bring.

She went to bed, leaving the sliding window open so that she could see the river flowing past. It made her feel safe, but she couldn't have said why.

Guinness Railwaybridge

Abren awoke in the morning to a high, tight whine which she'd never heard before. She leapt out of bed and followed it to Phaze II's room. Here she found him nursing his ear against the pillow, crying to himself through clenched fists. She went off for the Morgans, and found them in the kitchen bustling between the toaster and the frying pan. She told them about Phaze II and explained about the stampede at the football pitch. Sir Henry spat with disgust at the mention of the BC boys, and Pen rushed upstairs.

She was down again five minutes later, bringing Phaze II dressed and ready to be taken to hospital. He didn't want to go but didn't have much choice. Bright and determined, Pen whisked him away. Abren wanted to go too, but Pen said that she should stay. She bundled Phaze II into her car and the last Abren saw of them was when it pulled out into the steep lane which ran up from the river beside their house.

'Yet something else that's all my fault!' Abren said as she watched them go.

Sir Henry tried to coax her into eating some of the mountain of breakfast which was left behind. It was the last thing Abren wanted, but she gave in for a quiet life. While she ate, Sir Henry sat opposite her, drawing on a pipeful of his favourite smoke – dried coltsfoot, which he said grew down by the river.

Half hidden by its blue haze, Abren thought that he

did indeed look like a bold Sir Henry Morgan, with his clay pipe, wild curly hair and dark-brown eyes. Even more so when he got up, pulled on a pair of tall leather boots and turned towards the back door, announcing that he was off to see what he'd caught in his putcheons. Did Abren want to come with him?

Abren didn't know what putcheons were. Before she could ask, however, the door knocker thundered. Sir Henry went to answer it and a driver sat outside, blocking the road and yelling that he'd got a delivery for Mr Henry Morgan of Compass House, Town Walls.

'We'll have to look at the putcheons later,' Sir Henry called, rushing through the house to let the driver in round the back, and unload the deliveries down at the boat shed.

Abren was forgotten, much to her relief. Suddenly Compass House was empty, and she liked it that way. It was good to be alone, thinking her own thoughts. She didn't have to smile as if everything was all right. Didn't have to eat to keep anybody happy, or say she'd slept like a log in the marshmallow bed, when she would have been more comfortable on the floor.

She walked from room to room, exploring the house, but with her mind always on the phone. What was happening at the hospital? She wished that Pen would ring and tell her. Why had Phaze II cried like that? Was he going to be all right? In the end she sat down by the phone, wishing that she'd insisted on going along with them, and refusing to move until it rang.

How long she remained like that she didn't know. Only when the front-door knocker thundered again did she come to herself. She ran to the door, hoping it would be Phaze II, miraculously cured. But a police officer greeted her, standing on the narrow bit of pavement. She was a detective, she said, pulling out a wodge of official-looking papers, and she had some questions which she wanted to ask.

'You'll have been expecting me,' she said, walking straight in. 'You and your young friend. You'd better go and tell him that I'm here.'

Abren explained about the hospital, hoping that the woman would go away and come again another day. But she had a job to do and nothing, it seemed, was going to get in her way.

'Never mind,' she said. 'I can make a start with you.'

She marched into the Morgans' front room, bringing with her a hint of stale tobacco, settled down on the sofa and spread her papers around her. Abren sat on a wooden chair, as far away as she could get. The woman's job might be to ask questions, but Abren had spent months avoiding them, and she was determined not to change.

She wriggled on her chair, wishing herself anywhere but there. The woman stopped fiddling with her papers and briefly looked up. A pen sat poised between her brown-stained fingers. Abren looked into her cold eyes and longed for rescue.

'*Name, please,*' the woman said, bending over her papers again.

Abren refused to answer.

'*Date of birth?*'

She didn't have an answer.

'*Home address?*'

What could Abren say? She blushed, but remained silent.

'School? Brothers? Sisters? Home town ...?'

Abren sighed and shook her head. The woman sighed too, looking up again and tapping her pen up and down.

'All right, let's start again,' she said, her forehead wrinkling into a frown. 'It's important that we understand each other, you and I. You have a name. I want to know it. You have a date of birth, and a home somewhere and a family. A mum. A dad. An uncle or an aunty. A guardian maybe. Or a social worker. There must be somebody who's missing you. Little girls don't just appear out of thin air! So let's start again, shall we? From the top. Tell me your name. Come on. It's not too much to ask. Just a name for a start.'

She tried to smile – an expression worse even than her frown. Abren longed again for rescue, and suddenly Sir Henry appeared. He came through the door carrying a tray of coffee things.

'Here we are,' he said. 'I hope you haven't started without me.'

He poured the coffee, splashed a bit of rum in it for himself, and settled down between them like a referee. Abren turned towards him, her eyes pleading for help. The woman turned too, holding up her empty papers as if they spoke for themselves. There was little she could do to trace anybody's family without information, she said. A first name wouldn't hurt, just for a start.

Sir Henry looked at Abren. 'Surely a first name wouldn't be too much to ask?'

The woman's eyes bored into Abren. Abren blanched. Panic dried out her mouth. 'My name ... I mean ...' She took a deep breath. 'My name's – *Guinness,*' she said, grabbing the first name that came into her head.

'Guinness,' the woman said. Her voice was frosty. She wasn't smiling any more. She didn't write the name down on the form. 'And do we have a surname, dare I ask?'

'Er, yes – *Railwaybridge,*' Abren said.

'*Guinness Railwaybridge.*' Again the woman didn't write anything down. She plainly couldn't see anything to laugh about – unlike Sir Henry, who had to turn away. 'And can you tell us anything about yourself?' she said, making an effort to keep her voice even. 'A birthday? A holiday with your family? A favourite memory?'

Abren didn't answer this time. She didn't dare. The three of them sat in silence. 'Is there *anything* that you'd be prepared to tell us about yourself?' the woman said at last.

'Can't think of anything.'

The woman packed up all her papers. Perhaps she'd had special training to know when people were wasting her time. Or perhaps she could just tell anyway. Pausing only long enough to waft stale tobacco over Abren, she left the room saying she'd come back another time. Sir Henry saw her out. Abren listened as they stood in the hall, talking in low voices. Then the front door closed and the woman passed the window, heading along the town walls.

Sir Henry returned to clear away the coffee things, only to find Abren still sitting on the chair, staring at the empty sofa.

'I'm sorry. I shouldn't have upset her. Now she's angry, and it's all my fault,' Abren said.

'It's not entirely your fault, you know,' Sir Henry said. He looked down at Abren, and she found herself blushing. 'Sometimes other people are to blame too, and sometimes no one is. But the thing that really matters, at least for now, is that you know you're safe. And you are, you know. *You're safe with us.*'

As if he'd said enough, he passed out of the room, carrying the tray. In a moment of gratitude Abren felt as if she would have followed him to the ends of the earth. But she followed him into the kitchen instead, and here an unexpected smell greeted her, driving everything else away. Pungent and rivery, it came from the stove.

Abren wrinkled up her nose. Sir Henry grinned.

'Look what I found in my putcheon,' he said, nodding at the cooking pot. 'Tonight's supper. You can help me bake it. It's eel pie.'

'It's *what*?'

Sir Henry took the lid off the pot. Inside Abren caught a glimpse of something dark and shiny, poaching in cider vinegar.

'I couldn't possibly,' she gasped.

'There's no such thing as *couldn't possibly*,' Sir Henry replied. 'Particularly when you're worried silly – and don't tell me that you're not – and need to take your mind off things!'

He took an apron and tied it round Abren's waist, then took another for himself. As a means of taking her mind off things it was remarkably effective! It was only after the eel had been chopped and seasoned, laid out in a squidgy mess in the pie dish, covered with green herbs, rings of leek, soy sauce, little bits of ginger and Abren's pastry, that her thoughts returned to Phaze II. She glanced at the phone. Why didn't Pen ring? How was Phaze II? Was he all right, or was something dreadful wrong with him?

Suddenly she realised that Sir Henry was watching her.

'What is it?' she said, wondering if he'd heard something but was keeping it to himself. 'Why are you staring at me like that?'

Sir Henry laughed, deep in his eyes. 'I was just thinking that if your name's Guinness Railwaybridge, then I'm the real Sir Henry Morgan!' he said.

Abren laughed too, full of relief. 'If you must know, my name's Abren,' she confessed.

'*Abren.*' Sir Henry looked impressed. 'Well, well, well, so you're a river girl!'

Abren didn't have a clue what he meant, but before she could ask the back door swung open and Pen came in – without Phaze II. There was no cause for alarm, she said. He'd had some x-rays, and everything seemed fine inside his head. But his ear still ached, and the hospital had decided to keep him in overnight, just to be on the safe side.

Abren couldn't make out whether that meant that he was all right or not. But no one seemed unduly worried. Sir Henry made Pen a fresh pot of coffee, then disappeared down to his boat shed. Pen sniffed the air and glanced at the oven, and Abren told her about the eel pie.

They ate it for supper, and it turned out to be surprisingly tasty, washed down with port wine and mashed potatoes. When he'd finished eating, Sir Henry went back down to his shed. Pen sent Abren after him with a thermos of coffee. 'In case he's planning to work into the night,' she said.

Abren found Sir Henry crouched on the wooden-slatted jetty, painting black stuff on the upturned bottom of a little boat. He thanked Abren for the coffee, but didn't stop to drink because he wanted to get finished. Abren found a second brush and helped him. The boat was shaped like a nutshell, made of wooden lathes with canvas stretched over them. Once everyone would have travelled about in vessels like these, Sir Henry said. The squire to visit his neighbours, the local traders to peddle their wares, the preacher to visit the chapels on his circuit and the local poacher to bring home his ill-gotten game.

Coracles, they were called.

'They've been on the river since the dawn of time,' Sir Henry said. 'But most of them have gone now. And not just coracles, but river punts and ferries and old upriver trows. And the men have gone too – the river men who earned their living on the waters. And now they're lonely waters. A tame river, not a working one. And all that's left for us to do is read about the old days and wonder what it was like.'

Sir Henry sighed. Abren remembered what he'd said about her being a river girl, and wanted to ask him what he'd meant. But he got up as if he'd had enough for one night. He hadn't finished painting, but he'd do it in the morning, he said.

He turned to go. Abren looked at the water flowing past. It was hard to imagine a busy, working river on a night like this, with the water calm, not a hint of a breeze and nobody in sight.

'What's its name?' she asked.

'Whose name?'

'*Its* name – the river's.'

'She's not an "it". She's a "she". And she's called the Sabrina Fludde,' Sir Henry said.

The comfort blanket

Abren couldn't sleep that night. She lay on her marshmallow mattress and the river's name rose before her eyes. The *Sabrina Fludde*. She thought of Old Sabrina in her room under the bridge. Was it a coincidence that she and the river shared a name, or was there a connection between them – some special reason why Phaze II had called her its queen?

Abren tossed and turned, cursing Phaze II for being in hospital instead of here to answer her questions. And what about her own name – the one Sir Henry had said meant she was a river girl? Unable to get to sleep, Abren reached for her little blanket. But she couldn't find it in the bed, and it dawned on her that she hadn't seen it last night either. Not here, close to hand, nor anywhere else since coming to Compass House.

'I must have left it under the railway bridge. The only thing I really own – all I have from my old life! *How could I?*'

Abren lay rigid, her arms empty. Suddenly her bed felt harder and colder than the camp bed had ever done. It felt like a prison cell. She couldn't sleep without her blanket. She had to have it. To smell its special smell and feel its feathery edge against her cheek. *And she had to have it now!*

'Tomorrow just won't do!'

Abren got dressed, crept past Pen and Sir Henry's

118

door, taking comfort from the fact that she could hear them snoring, crept downstairs and slipped out, leaving the front door on the latch.

Outside she found the town walls silent, not a car or house light in sight. She headed for the railway bridge, taking the quick route across town rather than the long one following the river. She passed the high town cross and plunged down the road between the library and the castle, reaching the station to find its sliding front doors locked and its forecourt empty. The taxi rank was empty and the station's windows were dark.

Abren stared up at them, feeling foolish. Why couldn't she have waited until morning, she asked herself? Waited until she could have told Pen and Sir Henry about the blanket, and then they could have helped her find it? Why did everything always have to be a secret? Why couldn't she ever trust anybody? And why was she always running off?

With no answer to her questions, Abren started up the footpath between the station and the castle. She was sure that the side gate would be locked, just like everything else. But when she tried it, she found it open. Maybe nobody ever came up this dead-end path any more, or maybe the gate had been forgotten, just like the waiting rooms beyond it.

Whatever the reason, Abren slipped through the gate and started down the platform, heading for the Guinness hoardings. She couldn't see the old abandoned station rooms behind them yet – couldn't even see their roofs and chimney pots – but she could feel them waiting for her.

She reached the end of the platform, where railway

tracks snaked off into the distance leaving Pengwern behind. Only yesterday Abren would have seized the chance to follow them to Birmingham or London, but now all she could think about was her blanket. Nothing else mattered – nothing felt as real to her as embroidered flowers and birds, rivers and mountains, streets and houses, trees and boats. Nothing as real as a feathery edge against her cheek and a knot under her chin.

Abren reached the hoardings and squeezed between them. The waiting rooms sat at the bottom of the bank, dark and hidden, with the river running underneath them. There was no hint of light down there, but there *was* a twist of woodsmoke rising from a chimney pot.

Someone was at home in those waiting rooms, hiding in the darkness! *And that someone had to be Old Sabrina.* Abren stared at the smoke, glad that the old woman hadn't stumbled on the girders and fallen to her death, but wishing her anywhere but here – at least for now. She slid down the bank and started looking for a way in that wouldn't bring them face to face.

Finally she found it, squeezing through a broken window into the toilet, then making her way into Phaze II's room, looking for the light switch. But the moment she started across the room, she knew that something was wrong. And when she found the light, she realised what it was.

Everything had gone. The bags and boxes on the floor, the horse-hair mattress and the blankets, the camp bed and the plastic icicle fairy lights. Even the stacks of china cups had gone, and the tea bar had been yanked off the wall, leaving only a row of gaping holes.

Abren could have cried. Not just because she couldn't see her blanket in this room swept clean of everything. But for Phaze II. Once this bare, dark place had been a home – maybe not most people's idea of home, but his all the same. But now if he ever wanted to come back, he'd have to start again. Start turning nothing into something, always knowing that someone might come back and destroy it again.

Sick to her stomach, Abren turned away – only to find herself standing in front of the door to Old Sabrina's room. She caught a whiff of woodsmoke coming from it, and imagined the old woman in the ruins with not even a chair to sit on, staring at the door as if she knew that Abren, yet again, was to blame.

Abren felt even more sick. She would have run away if she could, but something drew her to the door. She peered around it – only to find that everything was as she had left it. *Exactly the same!* The carpets on the floor, the piano with its polished brasses, the mirror with its gilt frame. Even the chandelier with its cut-glass droplets was the same, and so was the marble fireplace. Old Sabrina's chair was pulled up in front of it, and the only difference was that a fire now burned again in the grate – *and old Sabrina had returned*.

Abren felt herself turn cold all over. What had kept this grandeur safe while even the chipped cups been taken from next door? Why had all these treasures been left behind, and what did the mysterious Old Sabrina have to do with it all?

Abren turned and fled, stumbling her way back through the toilet window and out on to the old track. She scrambled up the bank and, as if something was coming after her – old and terrible with birds'-nest hair and swollen feet – Abren tore between the hoardings and along the platform, heading back to Compass House without daring to look round or stop.

Even when she reached the house, she didn't feel safe. She slammed the door behind her and shot the bolts, glad for iron studs and thick stone walls. Then she ran up to her bedroom, rammed a chair under the door handle and climbed under the bedcovers. And even then she didn't feel safe, tossing in the bed as she asked herself, who *was* this Old Sabrina who never looked in anybody's face, who shared the river's name, and who sat like a queen, with powers of enchantment to keep the world at bay?

It was a question that nagged Abren for the rest of the night as she lay sleepless without the comfort of her blanket.

What swans do

In the end Abren must have fallen asleep because when she heard the screaming she thought that it was a dream. Only when she awoke properly did she realise that it came from outside. It was morning. The light was seeping coldly through her windows – and something terrible was happening.

Abren tumbled from her bed and tore out on to the balcony. And there beneath her on the river, in the grey morning light, a pair of swans were locked in battle. It was they who were doing the screaming. Their necks were knotted in mortal combat, and the bigger swan was winning. It was flapping at the younger one, churning up the waters as it tried to get on top of it. Tried to drown the younger swan by biting it and holding it down. And the younger swan was fighting bravely, but it was losing. The bigger swan was screaming in triumph, but the younger swan was screaming for help.

And Abren cried in answer, 'I'm coming! *I'm coming! OH, I'M COMING!*'

She tore down through the house without bothering to get dressed. Why the two swans were fighting, she didn't know. All she knew was that the younger swan was screaming for her. Through the kitchen she tore, past Pen who called, 'What's going on?', and down the terraced garden, praying not to be too late. Finally, she reached the jetty.

And she was too late.

Abren watched, horrified. The bigger swan was right on top of the younger one, holding it down with the full weight of its body. It was thrusting the young swan's neck under water with its hissing beak. The young swan's struggles were getting weaker and weaker. Abren sensed it giving up.

'You can't!' she cried. 'You've got to live! You've got to fight! *Fight for your life!*'

Scarcely knowing what she was doing, Abren went to jump into the river, slippers, pyjamas and all. It meant everything to her that the young swan should live. She couldn't have explained why. It just did. Before she could do anything, however, Sir Henry came tearing down the garden in his dressing gown.

'What d'you think you're doing? Get back from there! Don't you know how dangerous swans can be?'

He tried to grab at Abren but she tore out of his grip, yelling, 'I don't care if they're dangerous! We can't just let them kill each other!'

'We can't change nature!' Sir Henry yelled back. 'It's territorial – they're always killing off their young! It's what swans do!'

What swans do! Abren braced herself to plunge into the water, regardless of Mr Henry Stupid Scud-Morgan. She would have separated the swans with bare hands if she had to, but Pen came rushing down the garden too, clutching a broom. She thrust the two of them aside and had a go herself, getting the broom between the swans and trying to prise them apart.

But by now it was far too late. Abren turned away – she didn't want to see the young swan floating limply on the water and the bigger one gliding off, its neck held high as it hissed in triumph. She started up the garden. Pen called after her, 'Abren – *Abren*, are you all right?' But Abren didn't answer. Sir Henry called as well, but she couldn't trust him any more. He'd been her friend, her bold Sir Henry, but he'd stood aside and let it happen.

Abren began to cry – not with tears that anyone could see, but deep inside. There was more to what she'd seen than just a swan fight, dreadful though it was. She reached the house and slammed the door behind her. There was something deeper here. Something personal. She had remembered something, hadn't she? *Another terrible half-memory.*

Abren crept upstairs, bowed beneath the weight of her hidden past. She barricaded herself in her room, as if a chair under the door handle could keep her memories at bay. She refused to open up when Pen came knocking. Refused to answer when Sir Henry came too, calling through the door that he was really sorry for what he'd said – that he hadn't meant it to come out that way.

Abren didn't care what he'd meant. She lay on the bed, staring at the red paper banners. There were no sweet dreams for her, whatever they might say, only a nightmare which started with her name and ended with the memory of a hand upon her neck, pushing down, down down. A nightmare which had brought her to this town and trapped her in it. And now her memories were stalking her. She couldn't get away from them, however hard she tried. They were even here, at the door.

Downstairs, Pen and Sir Henry started arguing. Pen

wanted to try again with Abren, but Sir Henry wanted to leave her alone. Abren would talk to them when she was ready, he said. And all the more so if they didn't force the issue.

He must have won because Pen went out, taking the car, and Sir Henry went down to the boat shed where Abren heard him drilling and hammering. She was on her own again. She stared at the doorknob, feeling a fool. Nothing was beyond that door, waiting to get her. What had been the matter with her? She removed the chair, and the landing was empty, of course. She started down it, opening doors as she went just to prove the point.

But no matter how many doors she opened, the sense of being stalked wouldn't go away. It was ridiculous, of course, but Abren never knew where another half-memory might be waiting. She even checked outside the front door, armed with Sir Henry Morgan's cutlass, which the plaque beneath it said had been a killing implement in its day.

But nothing nasty lurked outside on the pavement and standing, clutching a cutlass blunted with the lives of men, Abren felt a fool. The things she feared most could never be held at bay – not even by the sharpest weapon. They weren't outside the door. *They were in her mind*.

But Abren clutched the cutlass all the same, returning into the house and roaming through it like a pirate on the night watch. She checked round every door – and there were plenty of them in Compass House! Behind them she found shelves crammed full of books, baskets full of ironing and dirty washing, windowsills full of model ships, tables full of paints and brushes, walls full of maps. And everywhere she went, like a theme which held it all together, she found old photographs.

Compass House was full of them. Many were of Pen and Sir Henry having fun, looking young and growing up. But some were of the river. On one wall Abren found an old man sitting in a coracle. On another she found a square-rigged little boat which reminded her of the embroidered one on her missing blanket.

She found it again later, on the cover of a book. She picked it up and turned it over. The book was about Pengwern, with pictures comparing the old town with the new. Abren started thumbing through, fascinated by the changes, reading snippets of the town's history as she went along.

Behind the boring stuff about medieval drainage, Elizabethan traffic problems and trouble with the high street's sinking cobbles, she found a town she'd never known existed. Right here in this town, there had been plagues and fires, fairs and masques, power struggles and bitter feuds. There had been great battles. There had been betrayals. There had been fortunes made by merchants whose family names still remained in the town's forgotten mansions. There had been hangings and fights. Incarcerations in the debtors' gaol. Moments of horror in the town infirmary, and moments of healing too.

All human life was here, and all human death. *And the river wove its way between it all.*

Abren stared long at the book. Finally she went to put it aside and it fell open at a page with an illustration. A watercolour girl stared up at her from a watercolour river where she leapt over waves as white as wild horses.

And the girl was Abren.

Abren stared at the page, scarcely able to believe what she was seeing. But the girl was her, without a doubt. She had her black eyes, her face and even her little shift-dress. And tied around her shoulders, with the jade-green river washing over it, she even had her little comfort blanket. And underneath it all, daubed in bold black letters, was the title of the painting:

RIVER SPRITE

Abren was still staring at the book when Pen came in. She called that she'd brought Phaze II home, but Abren didn't hear her.

'Are you all right?' Pen said, sticking her head round the door.

Abren didn't see her either. She had closed the book, but she could still see the girl. She mightn't look like her to anybody else, but Abren knew who she was. This was more than just a memory. *It was the truth about herself.* Maybe she only glimpsed it from afar, but there was a story in that girl's black eyes – and one day she would know it! A story in those waves like wild white horses. A legend waiting to be found, *and the legend was hers.*

'I said are you all right?' Pen asked again.

'I'm fine,' Abren replied, but she clutched the cutlass tight.

In the library

Later, Abren went in search of Phaze II. She found him almost unrecognisable, with scrubbed skin, shampooed hair and new clothes. He smelt of hospitals and looked like an ordinary boy. It was as if the stuffing had been knocked out of him. He wasn't a wild boy any more, slipping through the darkness in his ragged black coat. Nor was he the nearest Abren had to a friend, propping her up when she was sick, making her eat when she didn't feel like it, living through the winter with her when she scarcely knew that she was alive.

He was just a boy, who probably had a home somewhere, and a family and an ordinary life which he had run away from. He was a stranger.

'How are you feeling?' Abren asked awkwardly. 'Are you better now?'

Phaze II looked at her with his good eye. The other one was newly bandaged; he had medicine for his ear infection, antiseptic cream for his cuts and bruises and inhalers for his cough. He had an appointment to see a dietician about his strange toleration of the wrong sorts of food and his inability to hold down the right ones, and a specialist in bronchial diseases about his thin chest.

'In other words, I'm just fine!' he said.

They didn't speak again. What was there to say? They picked at their lunches in silence and avoided each other's eyes. Later, Phaze II half-apologised for being sharp with Abren. But she turned away. She would rather have a sarcastic Phaze II than a tame one, trying to be friendly because Pen had told him not to be so mean. She wanted the old Phaze II back again. The one who ran along the girders and was never afraid of anything.

In the end she left him looking like a lost puppy, hanging around the water's edge with Sir Henry, as if he didn't quite know what had happened to him. She went to find the book on Pengwern, but it had gone and for all her scanning the bookshelves and rifling desks and tables, she couldn't find it.

Abren turned back through the house, looking for Pen. But she had gone too, nipped out to the library, according to Sir Henry, with her stack of overdue books.

'She asked over lunch if you wanted to go too, but you didn't answer,' he said.

Abren borrowed Phaze II's coat, without bothering to ask, wrapped it around her as if it made her invisible, and sneaked across the town, head down like a fugitive. The library, when she reached it, was a massive, cathedral-like building with tall, arched windows and ceilings ornately ribbed and moulded. She lurked about in the main entrance, between old columns carved in stone, and a pair of statues in Elizabethan dress. A plaque in Greek and Latin hung over the door, and Abren hoped it didn't say that children were forbidden. Certainly children were going in and out, looking perfectly at home. Perhaps the words said 'Welcome'.

Abren plucked up her courage and slipped through

an electric door, which opened for her as if by magic. Inside she found no cold cathedral but a warm, bright fairyland. Appearances had yet again proved deceptive. She wandered along shelves bulging with books, videos, tapes and CDs. Past tables crammed with computers, aisles busy with borrowers, and nooks and crannies full of browsers tucked away for a good read.

All around her were arrayed thousands of books, and it was impossible to guess where the one on Pengwern might now be. So Abren started where she was, with 'Modern Lives', and worked her way through 'History', 'British History' and 'Military History', 'Geography of Britain', 'Architecture and Town Planning', 'Photography', 'Earth Sciences' and even 'Novels A–M and N–Z.'

But she couldn't find the book.

Even when she came across a section devoted to local history, she still couldn't find the book. Perhaps someone had taken it out again. One of the schoolchildren maybe, who were working at the tables with piles of books stacked around them.

Abren mooched along behind the tables, the black coat pulled around her tightly as she glanced over shoulder after shoulder. But the schoolchildren started noticing her, and turned round and stared. She returned to the shelves, rifling through them, trying to make it look as if she had as much reason to be here as anybody else. Suddenly, a librarian came walking straight towards her with a purposeful air.

Abren panicked. She was sure that the man was going to say, 'What are you doing here?' as if she were an intruder. But the librarian stopped in front of her and said, 'You look stuck. Can I help you?'

'I'm – I'm looking for ...' Abren lowered her voice, as if she didn't want anyone to know. The school-children were all staring at her, listening out for secrets which were hers alone.

'What was that? I didn't catch what you were saying,' the librarian said.

'I'm looking for ...' Abren swallowed hard. 'I'm looking for the history of Pengwern Railway Station.'

No sooner had she said it than Abren could have kicked herself. The librarian beamed, and marched off as if hers was an easy problem to solve. She followed wretchedly as he picked through shelves with all the enthusiasm of one who knew what she wanted and was determined to provide her with it.

She had missed her chance, hadn't she? What she really wanted was the next piece in the jigsaw story of her missing life. But what she got were histories of the railways, books on engineering feats, books on the industrial revolution and a crumbling old brown book on Pengwern as a commercial centre, without a single colour picture. The librarian poured them all into Abren's arms, and said that if she needed more she only had to ask.

She sank down at a table with the books piled around her. Where to make a start? The librarian could still see her, and so, wanting to appear grateful, she started thumbing through the books. Only when he'd gone did she dare get up to go, leaving them behind her in a pile. And as she did so, something fell out of one of them.

She stooped to pick it up – and found the next jigsaw piece after all! Not in the painting that she had come here for, nor in any of the books but on the floor! *Underfoot.*

It was a piece of paper. Abren opened it out. At first she thought it was a scribbled note on a page torn out of an exercise book, but then she saw that it was a schoolchild's poem, written in blue ink and marked in red with a top 'A' grade. 'Well done!' the teacher had written. 'This is an excellent poem for a boy of your age. I've read twenty-seven other poems on this theme alone, but yours will always linger in the memory.'

The poem's title was 'The Legend of Sabrina Fludde'.

High on Plynlimon, beneath stars,
Beneath black waters her body cast,
Her secret buried beneath mountain grass,
The hidden river knows her cruel past.

Forged in passion between king and maid,
With father's mortal beauty and mother's elven
*   gaze,*
With mother's elven wisdom and father's mortal
*   ways,*
Rich with all the gifts that love conveys.

Pengwern's princess, child of its great halls,
Light of its morning, carried on the dawn,
When the world was young by Effrildis born,
By Effrildis nurtured and from Effrildis torn

By vile Gwendolina, wife of Pengwern's king,
Who upon his child did vengeance bring,
Upon the maid Effrildis, the victor's sting,
Upon her husband's kingdom, sorrow and ruin.

Grieve for Pengwern, you silent witnesses –
Crows on rooftops in feathered mourning dress
Highways forlorn and forsaken palaces,
Walls that stand in abandoned emptiness.

Weep, you river where the child was cast,
Giving her name ABREN to the waters vast,
Corrupted to SABRENA now at last,
Giving her bright future to a bitter past.

When she'd finished reading, Abren folded up the
poem and pocketed it. She had found what she'd been
looking for all along. Found the legend, and found out
why Sir Henry had called her a 'river girl'. The only
wonder was that she hadn't come across it before.
Every child in Pengwern knew the story, it seemed.
Not just this unknown poet, but twenty-seven others
at the last count, and numerous others before that, no
doubt. Abren had thought her legend was a secret,
waiting to be found. But it was everywhere. It was
common knowledge. *It was even a subject for
homework!*

She pulled the coat around her and slipped away,
leaving the schoolchildren at their tables. Perhaps they
all were writing poems about the girl who'd given the
Sabrina Fludde its name. All imagining what it was
like to be Abren the elf-maid – not leaping over waves
as wild as horses, but sinking under them instead.

All the way to Compass House, Abren thought about nothing else. 'I couldn't possibly be that girl,' she said to herself. 'Not that Abren. Not her. It isn't possible to stop time moving on. I couldn't still be a child after all these years. Couldn't drown in the river, but not die. Couldn't drown centuries ago, and still be alive!'

At Compass House she couldn't face going in, so she took the lane down to the river. There it was sparkling like a band of diamonds beneath the bright afternoon sun. The swan fight was forgotten and a pair of curlews swooped over the water, calling to each other. A kingfisher darted past in a flash of gold and turquoise. A silver fish leapt and fell, creating rings of light, and a mother moorhen broke the rings with her chicks in tow.

Abren sat down on the bank, watching Canada geese with a string of goslings. *I couldn't possibly still be alive!* she said out loud. 'Not after all this time.'

But she knew she could. Before this river, anything was possible. This was a mother of all rivers, bearing every shape and form of life. A queen of rivers, and if anything could keep a girl alive – could keep her safe and bear her through the long years, bringing her back home – *then this was it.*

Abren reached into her pocket and brought out the poem. She read it again, then stared long into the water. The story *was* hers after all! She knew it was, deep inside. She was the daughter of Effrildis and the king of Pengwern. Was the Abren in the poem. But she hadn't drowned, like the poet had said. He'd got it wrong about that. The river had kept her alive. *Kept her through the long years, until now!*

Abren ran back to the house and let herself in. Voices mumbled in the kitchen, but she moved down the hall without noticing them. Old questions had been answered, but new ones were clamouring. Why had the river brought her back here, after all these years? And was it just her? What about the rest of them? Her mother, Effrildis – was she alive too? And what about her father? *And what about the jealous queen Gwendolina?*

Just as Abren's thoughts turned to the woman who had tried to kill her all those years ago, she reached the steps down to the kitchen. Voices rose to greet her, and she caught a whiff of smoke which didn't come from Sir Henry's coltsfoot pipe. Suddenly, she found herself transported back to Old Sabrina's waiting room. She remembered the woodsmoke and standing in terror before the old woman's door. And suddenly it was like a nightmare coming back to haunt her. She remembered tearing through the night town, never daring to look back, slamming the front door and bolting it, sticking a chair under the door handle and hiding under the bedcovers.

Now someone laughed down in the kitchen, and the nightmare became real. What if Old Sabrina had followed her that night? If she'd seen where Abren lived, and now she'd come to get her? If she were in the kitchen right now, talking and laughing as if she were an ordinary person? What if her old woman's face were a disguise, and underneath the wrinkled skin she was Queen Gwendolina?

Abren turned to tear away again – twice as fast as before, and never to come back. But Sir Henry heard her and came after her.

'Abren, don't go! There's someone here to see you! It's your friend from the police. She's got good news for you. In fact, it's brilliant, considering how much help you gave her. The police have found your family! Your mum and brother, and your family pets and schoolfriends and your old life. Guinness Railwaybridge – *you're going home!*'

Part Five
River Source

Blaen Hafren

On the last morning, Abren said a special farewell to the river. She went down to the jetty and watched it flowing slowly past. The morning was all dew and cobwebs and silver light. She sat on the jetty watching swans dabbling in the shallows, and said goodbye to the idea that she came from another life. Goodbye to the idea that she was a throwback from a legend, carried down the river through time, chased by some remorseless enemy, intent on revenge.

Phaze II opened the back door and called her in. What he thought about her leaving, she didn't know. They still hadn't talked, not properly.

'Breakfast's on the table,' he called. 'Pen says if you don't hurry, you'll miss your train!'

He didn't exactly look at Abren, and she didn't exactly look at him as she turned and left the jetty for the last time. Even more than when they'd left the railway bridge, the discoveries of this last week had come between them. This week of finding her real mother at last, and the answers to her questions. Of hearing about her flesh-and-blood brother, and about her school friends. Not friends she'd shared the dark with, like Phaze II, but friends she'd played and grown up with, whose families knew her and she knew them too.

And now here she was, walking up the garden for the last time, all dressed up in smart new clothes bought by her mother, not rummage clothes from Phaze II's bin bags. And as if he knew what she was thinking, Phaze II turned and went back inside.

Abren ate her final breakfast with her mother, who had stayed the night so that they could get away quickly in the morning. Pen made them sandwiches for the journey, and Sir Henry drove them all round to the station with suitcases full of luggage which Abren – who had come with nothing – had somehow managed to accumulate.

Her mother bought them all a coffee while they waited for the train. Abren stared at the old abandoned platform opposite. She could see the Guinness hoardings, but she couldn't see the chimney pots behind them. They belonged to another life – a limbo-life which had once been hers, but now she was herself again.

The train pulled in. Abren's mother opened the nearest door and Abren shivered at the thought of saying goodbye to Pengwern. Her mother shook hands all round, and Sir Henry helped to haul their luggage on to the train. Suddenly this was it – the moment of departure.

'Everything will be all right,' Pen whispered as she kissed Abren.

Abren didn't answer. She looked for Phaze II, but he had disappeared. Her mother called for her to get on board. Right down the train, doors were banging shut.

Abren followed her mother, still looking for Phaze II. Only at the very last moment did she see him. He was standing at the end of the platform, staring down the track. He didn't look in the direction of the old abandoned waiting rooms, and he didn't look at the train. Abren waved to him as it went past, shouting,

'Come and stay, won't you? Whenever you like.' But he showed no sign of having heard her.

The train pulled away, and it felt like a betrayal leaving him like that. The police had said that he, too, would have a family and they were working on finding it, as they had found hers. But Abren didn't believe them. *She* was Phaze II's family, just as he was hers. It was as strong as that – but she hadn't known it until now.

She leant out of the window, waving until the conductor told her to pull in her head. By now she couldn't see Phaze II any more, or the station, or the river. Couldn't see the town for a network of signal boxes, railway arches and tracks.

She found her seat and sat down. Her mother smiled nervously. She'd been chatty and excited all week, but the moment of departure seemed to have struck her dumb. Her hands twisted in her lap and her eyes slid out of the window as if she couldn't bring herself to look at Abren.

'I hope you don't mind travelling this way,' she said. 'We could have gone home in a police car, but I thought it would feel more special this way. More like a holiday.'

She had explained this before, but it was as if she didn't know what else to say. Abren looked at her mother – looked at her soft, wavy hair, so different from her own tangled mess, her powdery skin, pale lips and dove-grey eyes. They might be her mother's eyes, but they were a stranger's to her. But no one knew that – only Abren, staring at a face she couldn't remember.

Not that she had owned up, of course! Her mother

had wept when they had met. She'd clung to Abren crying, 'Oh, my girl, *at last*!' She'd hugged Abren tight, and Abren had hung her head, crying not with joy but with disappointment.

And now she hung her head again. Hung it to hide the truth that she still, after everything, didn't have a memory. She didn't even know where they were going, for all her pretending otherwise. All she knew about her old life was what she had managed to pick up.

Her mother started chattering again, filling in the awkward silence between them. It was a good job they'd got the sandwiches, she said. It was going to be a long journey, and they'd have to take Mr Morris's taxi at the other end as their poor old car had failed its MOT test. But Gwyn would be waiting for them, up at the turn-off. He'd been excited all week at the thought of seeing his sister again.

Abren tried not to panic at the thought of her brother Gwyn. She closed her eyes, but couldn't picture him. Couldn't remember anything about him. Her mother's voice droned on and on, as Abren leant back and let the rhythm of the train send her off to sleep. Things would be all right when she got home, she told herself. And at least she wasn't a child of legend. At least she didn't have to live with that! She was just an ordinary child, with an ordinary home which she would remember when she saw it.

Abren fell asleep, slipping into a world where she couldn't hear her mother's voice. Occasionally, she awoke to find landscapes that she didn't recognise slipping by under wide blue skies. At a halfway point they shared Pen's sandwiches and bought drinks from the refreshments trolley as it rolled past. Then Abren went back to sleep and didn't stir again until they arrived at their destination.

Here her mother had to shake her hard.

'Wake up, Abren. Come on – we've arrived! Don't just sit there!'

Abren stumbled off the train to find herself in a small country town, whose name she didn't recognise. All she knew was that it was as different from Pengwern as anything could be, with quiet streets and half its shops closed for lunch.

Abren's mother went in search of Mr Morris's taxi, and Abren went into a post office and bought a bar of chocolate and a postcard. She ate the one while writing the other to Phaze II. What she wanted was to invite him, again, to come and stay. But what she wrote instead was, *'I'm feeling frightened. Nothing seems right. Please don't forget me.'*

It was a strange message from a girl on her way home, who'd been so excited last night that she couldn't sleep. But Abren posted the card, just in time before her mother returned, riding in the oldest-looking taxi that Abren had ever seen. They piled on their luggage and climbed in, and the taxi set off down the street, over a small stone bridge where boys sat fishing, and out of town on a narrow, bumpy switchback of a road.

The road home. *At last.* Abren leant forward in the taxi, waiting for the moment of recognition, which would surely come. They drove through an oak wood, the sun shining through branches which were thick with new leaves. But her home wasn't down there among those mottled trees, and it wasn't in any of the farms and cottages which lined the road – some of them her friends' homes apparently, and her mother said they couldn't wait to see her again. It wasn't tucked away across fields, or anywhere else that Abren could see.

She started to grow restless. How much longer? she thought, but she had the sense not to ask.

Her mother glanced at her nervously. She had stopped chattering and an awkward silence fell between them. The further they travelled, the more it seemed to grow. Abren's mother's hands twisted in her lap. The taxi drove into a pretty hamlet comprising cottages, a farm, a school and an old stone church. The road sign announced Old Hall, and Abren found herself hoping that this would be her home. She saw a stream with a church set behind it, between rows of sloping graves. Shafts of sunlight shone upon tall arched windows and in one of them Abren glimpsed a face. It looked at her as she drove towards it, and Abren's heart began to pound. Did she know that face? Did it know her? Was it one of her friends, looking out for her?

The face was still there when the taxi left Old Hall, bumping its way over the brow of a small hill. Abren turned to take a last look and there it still was, a white face looking after her.

'Not long now,' her mother said, breaking their silence at last.

Abren shivered. Old Hall disappeared and the road ahead was dark with trees. These weren't golden oaks any more, but fir and spruce trees casting soft grey shadows. The taxi drove between them and the air turned damp and misty. Abren leant forward, hoping

146

that her home wouldn't be here. What she wanted was a bright house full of sunlight and white paint – somewhere like Compass House, not a dark house in a forest full of trees like soldiers guarding the road.

The taxi spluttered up between them, and Abren imagined it breaking down so that they would have to haul their luggage the last long mile to a horrid little house which she'd remember with dislike the moment she set eyes on it. To her relief, however, they emerged into a road which ran between a sunny glen and a disused quarry, completely overgrown.

The taxi drove up past this quarry and drew to a halt.

'This all right for you?' the driver said.

Abren's mother nodded, but Abren couldn't see a single house anywhere. Her mother got out of the taxi and started unloading their luggage. Abren got out too. Her mother paid the driver and he turned the taxi round and started back the way he'd come. Abren watched him disappearing back into the forest. Now they were on their own. The glen stood silent.

'What are we doing? I don't understand.'

Abren couldn't but ask, even if it gave the game away. Her mother turned and looked at her, and for a moment Abren thought that she was going to have to own up about not knowing where she was. But then a vehicle came lurching down a track which joined the road, and her mother said, 'What are we doing, indeed! Gwyn should have been here waiting for us, but he's late as usual. Look at him!'

The vehicle pulled round in the road – an old Land Rover whose cough and splutter made the taxi sound healthy. Behind the wheel sat a boy in dungarees and a checkered shirt. He was older than Abren, had the same untidy hair, and their mother's eyes. Abren's brother Gwyn, obviously.

He drew to a halt. Abren looked at him, her heart thundering. He nodded tersely, and she smiled back. Then he smiled at their mother, and something fleeting seemed to pass between them, without words. She went and hugged him. Neither of them said anything. Quickly and efficiently they loaded the luggage into the Land Rover, then they climbed in, setting Abren between them on the front seat.

They started up the track, travelling in silence. Abren looked at her brother's face. She didn't recognise it. Didn't recognise anything about him at all! Her own brother – but she might never have set eyes on him before!

It was a sickening moment for a girl who'd banked so much on getting home and finding her memory. Abren watched the landscape in trepidation as the Land Rover spluttered up the track. This was the landscape of her home, but its dark trees and plunging drops, grassy meadows and little streams meant nothing to her. She might never have seen those grazing sheep, or those browny-red birds wheeling in the sky, or those old boundary walls.

The Land Rover carried on, like an instrument of torture. Abren tried not to panic, but failed miserably. What if she reached journey's end and still didn't recognise anything? Not her home, nor her mother, nor her school friends, nor anything at all about her old life? The game would be up, and she'd have to confess. But, worse than that, she'd have to face a life without a memory. Without a childhood and a past.

With nothing but what she had now.

Slowly, the Land Rover pulled round a great sweep in the track. Ahead of her Abren suddenly saw an ivy-covered ruin with tumble-down barns behind it. The Land Rover drew close to them, and to Abren's surprise she saw curtains at windows and pots of geraniums on sills. Smoke was rising from a chimney. It wasn't a ruin after all!

It was her home!

Gwyn drove into a yard between the house and the barns. 'Here we are,' he said, relief in his voice. 'Back at last. Back at Blaen Hafren.'

Abren stared at the house, and couldn't move or speak. She waited for the moment when it would all come flooding back. But Blaen Hafren stared back in silence. It was just some old ramshackle farmstead, stuck up a track. It was nowhere special.

Nowhere that Abren remembered.

The mountain man

Abren sat in her bedroom, surrounded by luggage. Her mother brought up the last bag and dumped it down, then left the room, pulling the door behind her as if she knew that something was wrong and that Abren wanted to be alone with her thoughts. Her footsteps faded on the tiny winding staircase, and the house fell silent.

Abren sniffed the air as if she'd never smelt this musty bedroom before. Her own bedroom – but it felt as strange to her as the bedroom in Compass House. As strange as the railway bridge had felt when Abren had first gone there. As strange as that first night on the Bytheways' sofa-bed.

It was as if Abren had never smelt this musty air before, or seen the old oak beams and dipping floorboards of her bedroom. Never sat at this dressing table with its speckled mirror, or washed at this marble dresser with its jug and bowl. They could have been museum exhibits. They didn't feel like a part of her life.

She turned away, her expression grim, and started unpacking. Each item, as she brought it out, told more of a story than anything in this room. Underneath the new clothes which her mother had brought her were gifts which the Morgans had pressed on her. Soap and towels from the blue-and-white bathroom, books from their shelves, banners full of sweet dreams,

which had once hung over her head. And last of all –
completely unexpectedly –

'*Sir Henry Morgan's cutlass!*'

Abren lifted it out. The cutlass had been wrapped
carefully in layers of paper and a note had been
attached to it, which read, '*Never be afraid again – All
our love, Pen and Henry.*'

A lump formed in Abren's throat. It had been their
only pirate treasure, but they had given it to her.
Gently she removed the paper. The cutlass gleamed in
the afternoon light – cold steel, and scary, too, even
though Abren knew that if she put her finger on the
blade, the edge would be blunt.

Abren wrapped it up again, and put it in a drawer
with clothes on top, as if it were a special secret,
belonging to another life. Then she sat on the bed and
wondered at herself. What sort of girl was she, whose
memories began and ended in Pengwern? What sort of
girl, who could forget her family and her old life? She
felt ashamed. Blamed herself, yet again. Felt hot and
panicky and sick.

Suddenly, as if she couldn't stand her musty
bedroom any more, Abren jumped up. She had to go
outside, breathe fresh air, get away on her own.
Perhaps then, without her mother watching her, and
her brother staring awkwardly, as if not knowing
what to say – perhaps only then would everything
come back.

Abren hurried through the house, trying to work
out how to tell her mother that after months away, all
she wanted was to be alone. But she never had to. Her
mother was out in the back pantry having words with
Gwyn. She didn't notice Abren slipping outside,

crossing the yard, finding the stream which ran down the back of the house, and walking up beside it, lost in thought.

Abren walked until she found a waterfall, which she didn't remember, just like everything else. She clambered up beside its pools, shoots and gulleys, and found herself on the edge of the forest. Shadows fell across her, and she felt small beside the great trees. Felt like a nobody. A nobody without a memory.

Abren started up between the trees, climbing over roots and fallen logs, scrambling up a carpet of pine needles and following a path cut by the stream. Time passed, but she didn't notice until she emerged on to a vast open grassland, with the sun lowering in the sky. She looked at hills rolling off in all directions, and valleys fading into the night. The view stretched for miles, and she suddenly realised that it was no ordinary hill that she had just climbed.

It was a mountain. And what a mountain, too! Abren heard a symphony of breezes rippling through the long grass, birds singing their goodnight songs and dogs barking up ahead of her somewhere. She looked at tall reeds and bright mosses, stretching away like a sea that carried on for ever. And she saw the world beyond her, hill after hill and valley after valley, spreading out like a vast blue shadow which had no end.

Abren gazed at it all, completely mesmerised. It was only when the sky darkened and the rim of the forest faded with the light that she realised how late it was. She turned back, looking for the stream which was her only path home. Suddenly, a man appeared in front of her, looming out of the fading light.

Abren had thought she was alone up on the

mountain, but the man straightened up from a smoky fire which wrapped itself around him like a grey cloak. A pack of dogs played at his feet – steel-grey dogs with strange red spots. Perhaps they were the dogs that Abren had heard earlier. He waved a hand, and Abren waved back, taking in long leather boots, grass-green canvas trousers full of useful-looking camper's pockets, fiery gold-red hair and strikingly black eyes. A sky-blue shirt was open at the man's neck, and a chain hung round it, thick with silver charms.

Abren stared at the charms, and couldn't take her eyes off them. The man smiled.

'Are you lost?' he said. 'Out on your own?'

'I'm – I'm with my mother,' Abren said. 'She's just behind me.'

The man looked behind her, and the mountain was empty. Not a sign of anybody's mother. He smiled again. Looks like your mother has got lost,' he said. 'Where are you from?'

Abren didn't want to tell him, but she somehow couldn't help herself.

'I'm from Blaen Hafren,' she replied.

The man looked at her as if she weren't just mildly entertaining any more, but suddenly of real interest.

'Blaen Hafren?' he said, and his eyes seemed to tighten in his head. Like sharp black lenses they focused on Abren as if they hadn't really noticed her before.

'What of it?' Abren said.

The man shook his head. 'So the old girl's back. And so are you. The lights are on again, are they? *You must be Abren.'*

He took a step towards her and the dogs leapt out

153

of his way. His charms glinted at his neck, and Abren stared at them again. The man moved closer, holding out his hand.

'Don't be frightened,' he said.

Abren panicked and cried out. Immediately a sound came from the forest – answering as if on cue!

'Abren! *Abren* – is that you?'

Abren could have wept with sheer relief. 'It's my mother!' she said.

The man withdrew his hand. 'Oh, well,' he said. 'Tell her an old friend was asking after her. That he's glad to know the lights are on again at Blaen Hafren, and he's glad she's found her Abren. Tell her that we'll all meet soon, and that *her old friend hasn't forgotten her.*'

He kicked the fire. Through a cloud of ashes Abren saw her mother emerging from the forest. She waved frantically.

'You can tell her yourself! Here she comes ...'

She turned back – only to find that the man had gone. His dogs had gone too, and only the ashes remained, settling back on the cold ground.

Abren cried out. Her mother came up the open grassland, panting from her climb. Gwyn rushed ahead of her, and Abren flung herself at him.

'There! Just there! That man! *Did you see?*'

'See who?' Gwyn said. It was the first time he had spoken to Abren, and his voice was cold, as if he'd just about had enough of her.

'*That man!*' Abren said. 'You must have seen him. *That mountain man with his dogs!* I don't know how he did it – one minute he was here, and the next he was gone!'

Her mother came and joined them. 'What are you talking about? What man?' she said, resting her hands on her knees and struggling to catch her breath.

'He said that you were old friends,' Abren replied. 'He was glad to hear that the lights were on at Blaen Hafren. Glad that you'd found me, and said to tell you that we'll all meet up. Very soon, he said. Oh, and *he hasn't forgotten*. Whatever that means.'

Abren's mother turned to stone. At first Abren didn't notice. But when she turned to go, her mother remained staring at the ashes. She didn't know whom Abren could be talking about, she said in a cold stiff voice. Was she sure that she'd really seen someone? Sure that she wasn't making it all up?

Abren swore blind that she wasn't, and her mother shivered. Gwyn came and put a hand on her shoulder. Perhaps now they were here, he said, they should carry on to the top. He looked straight into his mother's eyes, as if he were trying to tell her something, but she turned her face away.

'Not tonight,' she said with sudden urgency in her voice. 'We've got to get back home. There's a storm on the way. Can't you feel it? If we don't leave now we'll regret it. Come on, both of you. Don't just stand there. *Hurry up!*'

Calling the corph candle

There *was* a storm. It lasted all night. The first few drops started falling as they made their way along the smooth top of the waterfall, and by the time they reached Blaen Hafren, rain was running down its roof in sheets. Gwyn slammed the door behind them and even bolted it, 'in case the storm blows in'.

Their mother made them supper – oven chips and greasy tinned beef. For a welcome-home meal it wasn't a patch on stew and dumplings, or even on eel pie! All the while they ate, the storm ranted overhead – an angry monster shaking Blaen Hafren within an inch of its life. Abren's mother listened to it with a long face. Rain came dripping through the ceiling and she sent Gwyn dashing about, catching it in buckets and bowls. She shuttered the windows and stuffed towels under the doors. But still it found its way in.

Abren suggested that they watch the television to take their mind off things. But her mother said it wouldn't work in a storm like this. Abren suggested phoning the Morgans, just to let them know that she had arrived. But her mother said that the phone line was down.

In the end, bored and restless, Abren went to bed. It was a funny sort of homecoming – not what she had hoped for. Downstairs she could hear her mother raking out the living-room fire and turning out the lights.

Abren closed her eyes and tried to sleep, telling herself that despite everything it was still good to be home. But the storm kept her awake and she tossed and turned, missing her comfort blanket more than ever. Slates slid down on to the front path, and rain found its way in, dripping round the bed. Abren told herself that the storm would soon be over. But her bedroom was freezing and damp, the ceiling was springing more leaks by the minute, and her windows were shaking fit to shatter.

Finally, unable to stand it any more, Abren got up, put on her newly bought dressing gown and headed downstairs, hoping there'd be a bit of fire left in the grate. She expected to find everywhere in darkness, but when she passed the kitchen door she found the light on and her mother sitting at the table.

Her face was turned Abren's way, but she didn't see her at the door. Abren stood behind it. There was something very still and solitary about her mother. Something almost bleak, which made her want to rush in, throw her arms around her and own up about her memory. It was as if it lay between them like a barrier, cold and awkward, and growing all the time – particularly since they'd arrived at Blaen Hafren.

But before Abren could do anything, Gwyn stepped out of the shadows at the far end of the room.

'I *still* say we don't know it's him,' he said. 'It could be anyone remembering the old days, and looking for lights on at Blaen Hafren! You shouldn't worry so much. It'll be all right. We've got her back, after all. And we're the ones who've done it – *not him!*'

The windows shook behind their shutters. Abren's mother tilted her head. 'Whose dogs are those, barking in the wind?' she said. 'You may not think it's him, but just you listen!'

Abren listened too, but she couldn't hear anything. Neither could Gwyn. He laughed at his mother. 'This is ridiculous!' he said. 'You're worrying about nothing. You'll see tomorrow, when everything's just fine. I'm off to bed ...'

Abren's mother let him go without a word, melting back into the shadows. She sat for a long time staring at the table and Abren thought about going to bed herself. Suddenly, however, her mother got up, an expression of determination on her face, fetched a bucket and a brush – and started scrubbing the table!

It was a strange thing to do in the middle of the night, in the middle of a storm, but she carried on until the table was raw. When she'd finished, she got a towel and rubbed it bone dry. Then she went into the cupboard and came out with something rolled up in a piece of red cloth. She laid it on the table, removed the string, which she wrapped around her wrist, and unrolled – a thick black candle.

'Let's see if tomorrow really will be *just fine*!'

Abren didn't have a clue what was going on. She watched her mother take the candle and set it in the middle of the table, go off and make herself a cup of strong tea, drink it down as if to steady her nerve, circle the table a couple of times, her apprehension plain to see, and finally light the candle with a long match, standing well back.

Immediately, a dusky, beautiful glow rose through the kitchen, transforming everything and shining into every corner. It lit up the dresser, the sink and the rugs on the quarry-tiled floor, and even the rainwater in the bowls and buckets. Lit up the shutters, and lit up Abren's mother, with her tight, pale face.

For a moment Abren's mother stared into the yellow light, then she leant across and blew out the candle. The glow disappeared as quickly as it had come, and the room looked tawdry in the ordinary light. But a single strand of smoke remained, rising like a wish. A secret smile crept over Abren's mother's face. There was no storm outside – only this. She watched the smoke reach the ceiling and start snaking round the room.

Abren watched it, too. As if it were a living creature, the smoke passed beneath the old oak beams, drifed over the dresser, coiled across the sink and wafted across the floor. It sniffed its way towards the door, and for a terrible moment, Abren thought it was going to seek her out. But it carried on round the room until it reached a bowl of rainwater under the far window. For a moment it lingered over the water. Then it sank beneath the surface and disappeared from sight.

Abren's mother sighed.

'Well, there it is.'

It wasn't she who spoke, but Gwyn, who hadn't gone to bed after all, stepping out of the shadows. 'Perhaps it *was* him, like you said. But tomorrow will be everything we wanted. He can't stop it. The corph candle's spoken. It's in the water, plain to see. This is our chance. A death by drowning – *at last!'*

No photographs

Abren awoke feeling troubled, but not knowing why. The sun was shining, the storm had gone and the morning outside her window was crystal clear. She stood looking down the long glen. All the way to the forest she could see sunlight and bright colours. It was a perfect morning. *So why so downcast?*

Her mother came into her room, singing a song. The storm had gone, she said, and it wouldn't be back. The weather had changed for the better, and she had promised Gwyn that they'd go up the mountain to their favourite picnic spot. There'd be no jobs about the house – not today. This wasn't an ordinary day. It was Abren's first proper day back home – and they were going to spend it celebrating!

Abren turned from the window and followed her mother downstairs to the kitchen, where she found Gwyn at the breakfast table.

'Good morning,' he sang out, as if the mood were a disease and he had caught it too.

Abren sat down opposite him and started eating. Their mother brought a knapsack out of the pantry and started packing it with their lunch. They were going to leave early, she said. Leave straight away and make a day of it.

'Hurry up with your breakfast, you two,' she said.

After breakfast, Abren asked about the phone. She wanted to ring the Morgans and speak to Phaze II, but her mother said that the line was still down. Abren tried not to be disappointed, but she would have given anything to hear Pen's voice. To know what Sir Henry was getting up to today. To find out if Phaze II was all right.

'Go and get dressed, *quickly*!' her mother called. 'Don't just stand there!'

She clapped her hands and Abren scuttled upstairs. Something felt wrong, for all the brightness of the morning, but she couldn't have said what. Only when she went to wash herself, pouring water from the jug into the china bowl, did she remember her dream. What a strange dream it had been, disturbing and mysterious! She stared into the bowl of water, and remembered her mother's face as she'd scrubbed the table clean; the way she'd prowled around the kitchen as if afraid to strike that match; the way the smoke had risen round the room as if it had a life of its own. She remembered Gwyn saying strange things which left her feeling funny inside. Things about water, and about candles speaking, and about …

A death by drowning!

That was it!

Abren stared at the bowl, seeing that other bowl, with the smoke sinking into the rainwater. Suddenly she felt sick. She stared around her, and her bedroom stared back – a cold room with no pictures on the walls to comfort her, not even a family photograph.

'*Come on, Abren!*' her mother called.

But Abren wasn't listening. Where *were* the family pictures? she asked herself. *Where were the photographs?* The Morgans had them everywhere, and so did Bentley and his family. Photographs of growing up and doing things together – of special moments and school events. And photographs of their uncles and aunts, cousins and grandparents, and of their friends too.

So where were Abren's photographs?

Why weren't they here?

Abren tore into Gwyn's room and found it bare too. There were no photographs, CDs, stereo, books, posters, clothes tossed in corners, old toys left over from his baby days, computer games or anything else.

What was going on here?

Abren ran on to her mother's room. Here again there were no personal things. No bills and letters lying about, no photographs or paintings on the walls, or dirty clothes in the linen basket. There *was* no linen basket, nor any other signs of ordinary family life.

Abren felt herself go cold all over. Suddenly, it felt as if this musty house had never been her home. She looked down at the bed. Her mother's nightdress lay on it, carefully folded over. A pair of shoes sat on the floor, and the clothes she'd worn in Pengwern hung over the wardrobe door. But that was all. There wasn't as much as a hairbrush on the dressing table – and when Abren leant across and started opening the drawers, *they were empty*.

She worked her way through them, quick and silent, waiting for her mother to call up the stairs yet again. Finally, she opened the last drawer – and there lay the black candle.

Abren stared at it, rolled in its red cloth. The string was missing – and she didn't need to ask herself where it might be. *It was wrapped around her mother's wrist!*

'It all really happened,' Abren whispered to herself. 'Everything from getting the candle out of the cupboard, to standing it on the table. And circling round the table, and striking the match, and leaning over and blowing it out. *It wasn't a dream.* The smoke really rose round the room, and Gwyn really said that thing about the death by drowning.'

Abren closed the drawer. She returned to her bedroom, the picnic forgotten. She didn't know what had happened downstairs in the kitchen in the middle of the night. Didn't know what it all meant, but one thing was for sure.

'Something's wrong. Very wrong. *I've got to get out of here.*'

Abren didn't dare go downstairs. Instead, she forced the window open, and clambered down the front of the house with the agility of a girl who could manoeuvre herself up and down girders in the dark. Her mother would be furious after all the trouble she had been through bringing Abren back to Blaen Hafren. But this wasn't Abren's home. She was sure of it. And something bad would happen if she stayed. *She was sure of it.*

Abren hit the track and didn't stop, tearing down it until Blaen Hafren was out of sight and she could see the road ahead. She headed for it at full pelt. Perhaps there was a simple explanation for everything that had happened – perhaps her mother could account for everything, if only Abren would wait. But she didn't dare to risk it.

She reached the road and started down the glen. A pair of red kites wheeled overhead, and sheep looked up from their grazing to watch her pass. Abren glanced behind. Nobody was coming after her yet. But they soon would! Her mother would go upstairs, fed up with waiting. Either that or she'd send Gwyn. They'd find that she had fled again, and then they'd come after her. Nothing would stop them. They'd be in the Land Rover, MOT or not, and the road wouldn't be safe any more.

Abren plunged into the forest, relieved to hide herself beneath its canopy of leaves. She ran until her heart was bursting and her legs were almost giving way. She wanted to stop and rest, but didn't dare. Her mind was a whirl. Nothing had been right since leaving Pengwern. It wasn't just the strange events in the kitchen last night. It was her mother too – something changed about her ever since they got on that train. And it was Gwyn as well, and the way he never smiled at her. And it was even the journey here – the whole long journey, bringing her to a place with no dirty linen in the basket and no photographs on the walls.

Now Abren tried to turn the journey on its head, running back to Pengwern, convinced that she could really get there if she only kept going. Behind lay everything that she had been led to believe was her old life, but ahead lay her real life – her life with the Bytheways and Morgans, with Old Sabrina and Phaze II and, most of all, *the river*.

The river she'd often longed to get away from, as if it held her prisoner! But now she simply longed for it. *And she would have it.*

Abren was determined. She would return to Pengwern, and nothing would get in her way. If there was a simple explanation for everything, then her mother could come and tell her there, where she felt safe. She could come for her again, and they could start all over. They could do it properly. No secrets this time. No funny goings-on in the kitchen at night. No swearing blind not to know people who sent their greetings and said that they were old friends.

Abren would explain about her memory, and her mother would explain about a *death by drowning*. She'd explain about the mountain man, and about the strange corph candle. Then, with Abren's friends around her, and in the safety of Compass House, she and she alone would decide what she wanted to do.

Abren ran out of the forest with a new sense of purpose. How she'd make those miles back to Pengwern, she didn't know. But she was on her way. And she would get there if she just kept on! There was a world beyond this mountain – a world that was her own, and she would find it!

She ran over the brow of a small hill. Ahead of her stood a cluster of stone buildings. She headed for them, stumbling into Old Hall.

Old Hall

Two bells rang every day in Old Hall. The first was the church bell, and the second belonged to the school – a stone building with walls as thick as a castle's and a big turf roof. Abren could hear the second now, ringing for breaktime.

She drew towards it, longing for a break herself. She had run and climbed, ducked and dived for hours, yet the weariness she felt went deeper than aching bones and muscles. She looked at the playground, set between trees, with children pouring out into it. Some of them were singing a song and Abren listened with envy.

Why can't I be like them? she thought. Why can't I learn the things I need to know by singing songs, playing games, learning lessons in a classroom with a turf roof? Not running like a crazy child through a world that's even crazier!

Suddenly the fight went out of her, and all she wanted was to rest. She turned away from the school, and her eyes settled on a grassy bank. It was set well back from the road, shaded by yew trees. Nobody would find her there if they came looking for her, she thought, not beneath those shaggy branches.

So Abren headed for it, wading through the stream and climbing out on to the bank, which was full of daffodils. She flung herself down and straight away fell asleep.

How long she stayed like that, stretched out flat upon the good earth, she didn't know. The sun moved between the trees, but she never noticed. Blackbirds sang to each other across the stream, but she never heard them. Never heard anything – until a voice awoke her.

'I'm sorry to disturb you, but I wouldn't stay here, if I were you. The bees might get you!'

Abren came to herself with a start. She lifted her head, and a woman dressed in a white space suit stood in a patch of sunlight between the yew trees, looking down at her. Over her head was thrown a ghost's white shroud, and in her hand was a tin can with a spout.

'*Bees?*' said Abren.

'All around you.'

Abren looked around and noticed the hives. They stood off the ground on stilts: tall tiered boxes, with bees drifting in and out between their wooden slats.

'And not just any old bees, you know,' the woman said. 'They're St Curig's bees. They've been collecting nectar from the mountain since the dawn of time.'

They looked like any old bees to Abren. She watched the woman putting on thick gloves. Obviously she was a bee-keeper, and this was her garden. Abren felt embarrassed that she had failed to realise it. Beyond the yews were flowerbeds and shrubs, deckchairs and gardening tools, baskets full of washing and yet more washing drying over bushes in the sun.

'I'm sorry,' Abren said, scrambling to her feet. 'I was just so tired. I didn't know that I was trespassing.'

She turned to go, but the woman called her back,

167

reaching out for her with a gloved hand. She raised her veil and a few bees settled on her face. But she didn't notice them, looking intently down at Abren.

'You poor child! You *are* tired! Why don't you come inside?' she said. 'The hives can wait till later. You look in need of amber tea.'

She turned and started up the garden, as if it had all been decided. Abren followed her past a row of headstones, which she hadn't noticed before. Suddenly she saw a church ahead of them, its tall arched windows draped with curtains, and pots of geraniums on its sills.

'I don't understand,' she said. 'Is this a graveyard? I thought it was your home.'

The woman smiled. 'It *was* a graveyard, long ago,' she said. 'But now, yes, it's my garden, and the church you're looking at is my home. Mine and my sister's. You can see her at the window. She's Miss Ingram, and I'm Miss Ingram too.'

Abren looked up at the church, and saw the face at the window that she had seen yesterday. It smiled at her between the geraniums, and Abren smiled back. The first Miss Ingram reached the big church doors, arched like the windows and carved with scrolls and leaves. She stood inside the porch removing her gardening shoes. Abren noticed a brass name-plate. ST CURIG'S HOUSE. INGRAM. NO HAWKERS OR CIRCULARS. GENUINE CALLERS ONLY, it read.

The first Miss Ingram took off her gloves too, and pushed open the big doors. Abren hoped she counted as a genuine caller. She passed through into a single, high-ceilinged room which might not be a church any more but still contained some pews, a smattering of stained glass, a shiny golden lectern shaped like an eagle, and rows of organ pipes.

Abren looked around while the first Miss Ingram peeled off her veil and suit, and hung them in a cupboard. The centre of the room was taken up with the biggest table Abren had ever seen. Upon it everything from home-made bread and cakes to books, and ironing, wine bottles and vegetables from the garden lay piled up in an untidy clutter. Sunlight shone upon them, making everything bright.

Abren walked round to the far side of the table, and a black stove with a wonky pipe came into view. It stood at the end of the room, above the old altar steps. Beyond it stood what might have been a lady-chapel, but was now a glazed conservatory. Here the second Miss Ingram sat surrounded by a clutter of yet more books, balls of wool in a basket, a row of plants in pots, jars of fermenting, golden liquid, an embroidered footstool and a small white dog.

'Come and join us,' the second Miss Ingram called, looking up from a sock which she was darning.

She cleared a seat and Abren crossed the floor to join her. She smiled as if Abren were an honoured guest, and carried on darning. A little pair of glasses sat on the end of her nose and her needle flew in and out of the woollen sock. She didn't say anything, and Abren sat down. The little dog made room for her and she gave it a pat. Before she could think what to say, the first Miss Ingram appeared with the promised amber tea. It shone like gold.

'Amber tea's our speciality,' the first Miss Ingram said, handing Abren a cup.

'*One* of them,' the second Miss Ingram corrected her.

'Made from mountain nectar,' the first Miss Ingram said, ignoring the correction. 'The very best. We use it here for everything from medicine to mead.'

Abren took the cup, which was made of white porcelain and looked fine enough to break at a touch. She sipped carefully and the Misses Ingram watched her, smiling as the tea went down. It tasted wonderful, sweet and rich and hot. When Abren finished, the first Miss Ingram poured a second cup.

'Have some honey cake as well,' she said.

Abren took a piece of cake, which crumbled in her fingers and was studded with chocolate chips, much to her delight. With every bite, she felt less daunted by the journey ahead. No longer did her bones ache. No longer did it matter if she learnt everything the hard way. *The fight was on again.*

She drained her second cup, ready to get going. The first Miss Ingram made her drink a third before she'd let her leave, and the second Miss Ingram produced a vial of mead wrapped in a twist of paper. She said it was a gift from the bees – to remind Abren that there were good things to be found, too, on Plynlimon Mountain.

Abren looked at the second Miss Ingram curiously, but she didn't elaborate. She just slipped the little vial of golden liquid into Abren's pocket, and the first Miss Ingram said:

'The bees have been our life's work. And the life's work of our ancestors before us, living here in Old Hall for more years than you could ever count. Nobody knows those bees like we do. And nobody knows the mountain like the bees. They know when it's at peace, and they know when trouble's brewing –'

She broke off, glancing at her sister as if to check that she hadn't spoken amiss. Her sister nodded, but didn't say anything. They both looked back at Abren. Dimly it dawned on her that they were telling her something.

'*What is it?*' she said.

'Take care on your journey,' the second Miss Ingram said. She adjusted her glasses and returned to her darning, as if she'd already said too much.

The first Miss Ingram started clearing up the tea things. 'Just a word of advice. Your safest bet is to keep to the stream.'

Abren took her leave of them. She turned back once, and the first Miss Ingram stood waving in the porch. Abren waved back. At the window she could see the second Miss Ingram stooped over her darning, her needle flashing in the sun. She didn't look up, and Abren turned away beneath the yews, wondering if they'd ever meet again.

She left Old Hall, keeping to the stream. In and out of its golden waters she ran, over smooth stones and between peat banks, around willow-fronded pools and over gravel shallows. Ahead of her lay the little town with the railway station. She headed for it, running without stopping, listening for her mother's car but never hearing it.

Finally, it started getting dark. Still Abren hadn't reached the town, and she started looking for a place of shelter, thinking that she'd rest for a few hours, then start again before first light. A barn looked promising, but farm dogs barked at her. A cottage looked empty, but it turned out to be inhabited.

In the end she found a willow island in the shallows

of the stream. The last light was fading as she waded out to it, and a breeze blew down from the mountain. It reminded her that winter wasn't over yet, just because of a few daffodils. She shivered as she dug among the willow roots, looking for her shelter. Night fell, and birds stopped calling to each other. The breeze dropped and the trees fell quiet.

The quietness wrapped itself around Abren, and she felt her spirit sink. Had she done the right thing in stopping for the night, or should she have carried on? It was lonely on the island, with only the stream for company, flowing off to its unknown destination. Scary, with her mother surely out there somewhere, trying to get her back.

Abren listened to the stream murmuring as it flowed into the darkness. She fancied that she heard something. A snatch of a new sound carried on the water. Just a whisper, but growing all the time – and Abren knew what it was!

'You're fine,' the stream sang sweetly. 'Really. Fine. You're brave and strong and where you should be. There's nothing to be frightened of. *Trust me.*'

Abren listened in astonishment. *It was 'her' tune!* The one she'd heard under the railway bridge, and again on Christmas night, played on Bentley's saxophone. Now here it was again. Here in this stream. As Abren listened, voices took it up. Phaze II's voice, and Pen's and Sir Henry's. Fee's and Mena's voices, and Bentley on his saxophone. The Chadman's voice – yes, even him – and the Buddhist boys out peddling tracts on Pride Hill. And the buskers' voices on the hill, and the beggars' too.

Abren heard them all. And over all of them, like the

leader of the orchestra, like its star prize turn, Abren heard the selfsame river that had brought her down to Pengwern through the cold October morning mist. She heard it in the little stream singing to her through the darkness, *and its notes were words, and every one of them a song of secret comfort.*

Somewhere off across the night a car moved on a road, its headlights bobbing in the distant darkness. But Abren never noticed. She was looking at the stream – *and seeing the Sabrina Fludde.*

Abren turned back to the mountain, which the second Miss Ingram had called Plynlimon, though she hadn't noticed until now. Plynlimon, which Phaze II had told her was the source of their river. It shone beneath the rising stars as if it were a perfect mountain, not one where trouble brewed, according to a few old bees.

'*High on Plynlimon Mountain, beneath stars,*' the schoolboy's poem had said.

Suddenly, Abren knew that there was only one river in her story.

'*One river, one story, one life.*'

In the darkness someone laughed. Abren turned to see a car parked on the bank between the road and the stream. Its headlights had been switched off, its engine was silent and leaning against it – as if he'd been waiting with relish for just this moment – stood Gwyn.

St Curig's bees

At first they fought each other, running through the stream and out again, kicking, stumbling, winning, losing, chasing and being chased until, finally, Gwyn grabbed Abren and dragged her into the Land Rover.

They drove in angry silence through the night. Stuck beside her brother, Abren blamed only herself. She'd got away but had wasted her chance. She'd been a fool and stopped to rest. And now here she was, on her way back up the mountain. The mountain where trouble brewed, according to the Misses Ingram.

Abren tried to tell her brother all about it. But he wouldn't listen. She tried to plead with him to let her go.

'What's it to you if I run off?' she cried. 'You'd be happier without me, I just know. You don't like me. I can tell.'

Her brother didn't answer, just changed gears. The road grew steeper. Farms and woods flew by and there was nothing Abren could do to stop them. They reached Old Hall and she willed the Misses Ingram to see her from their window. But the curtains of St Curig's church were drawn for the night, and the car passed through Old Hall without anybody seeing.

It turned up the mountain road, entering the forest. Abren tried again to reason with her brother.

'Why won't you listen when I talk to you?' she said. 'Is it because you're frightened? Frightened of the mountain man? Frightened of what he said? *Is that it?*'

Still Gwyn didn't answer, just drove on. Through the darkness he drove, through the shadows and up past the rows of trees ranked like night-watch soldiers. A little wind got up, running down the rows. The Land Rover coughed and spluttered, and Abren willed it to break down.

Again she tried with Gwyn, asking him about the coil of smoke which had sunk beneath the water, and the death by drowning. But it made no difference. He drove on through the forest in silence, his foot down on the accelerator and his eyes fixed straight ahead, never slowing until they came out into the road beside the glen.

Here the Land Rover began to cough again. It started slowing down and for a moment Abren caught a glimpse of light down in the glen. She guessed it was a cottage and turned to look after it as they drove past. There were other people down there. Other lives. A chance of ordinary human warmth. A chance of rescue, even.

But as quickly as it had come, the light was gone.

Abren started on at Gwyn again. 'Something's wrong. Very wrong. It's not just me who ought to get away. It's you, too! Something's going to happen on this mountain. *I know it is!*'

Gwyn carried on, as silent as ever. The Land Rover groaned, and he swung it off the road on to the track. By now a light mist was rolling down the mountain, and the bright stars were disappearing. Abren felt its clammy coldness seeping into the Land Rover. It felt like winter again. She dared herself to open the door and jump out, but the quarry plunged away into steep darkness on one side of her, and on the other ran a narrow gorge.

Abren shivered. She didn't stand a chance. She turned to threats instead.

'If you don't let me go, it'll always live with you! You'll always remember what you did to me! *It'll haunt you for the rest of your life!*'

Still Gwyn didn't reply, but he turned his head. Their eyes met, and briefly Abren saw anger and confusion, bitterness and fear, shame and naked hate. She looked away. It was all more than she could bear. She looked into the gorge – *and saw a light.*

Dim but glowing steadily, she was sure it was the same light she had seen before. But this time it was moving. She'd got it wrong about it being a cottage back there in the glen. Abren watched the light between the trees, sometimes half-hidden, sometimes plain to see, keeping its distance – but always there.

It was following them.

She almost cried out with relief – but managed to bite it back. Blaen Hafren loomed out of the night, drawing closer all the time. But the light had changed everything. Someone was out there in the darkness. Someone knew the trouble Abren was in.

The Land Rover turned into the yard and gave up at last. Abren's mother stood in the open doorway. Her expression was stony. No sooner had Gwyn opened the driver's door than she was thrusting him aside, reaching in for Abren and yanking her out. Her hands were shaking. Her mouth wagged up and down, yet nothing decipherable came out.

'I didn't mean ...' Abren cried. 'I know it looks as

if I only want to hurt you ... It isn't really that I want to ... It's just ... it's just ...'

She got no further. Her mother frogmarched her into the house, slammed the door behind them all and dragged her runaway daughter across the floor, crying, *'To your room, madam! And don't think you'll ever get away like that again!'*

She dragged Abren up the stairs, refusing to hear a word of explanation, thrust her into her room and locked the door. Abren ran straight to the windows, but they had been shuttered, and there were locks on the shutters.

She slumped down on the bed. A prisoner in her own home! Except that it had never felt like home. Never felt right – and never less so than now!

Abren turned back to the window, thrusting her face into the crack between the shutters. She was looking for the light, burning in the night to tell her that help was at hand. And she found it burning, all right! But it wasn't what she had expected.

It shone against the glass, close enough to touch. Close enough to warm the glass – and yet the glass was cold. Close enough to shine into the room, and yet the room was dark. And the light wasn't human and companionable. It didn't bring a chance of rescue.

It was the black corph candle.

Abren could see it clearly. The candle of death. The candle of *her* death. Her death by drowning, no less!

Abren leapt back from the shutters, stumbled through the darkness to the chest of drawers, rifled through the clothes and grabbed Sir Henry Morgan's cutlass. If anybody came for her, then they would get it! The cutlass might be blunt, but it had struck before, killing hundreds, maybe thousands, and *it would strike again*!

Abren sat all night with it cradled in her arms. Finally, she fell asleep, and when she woke up in the morning, it was still there.

She opened her eyes, and it was the first thing she saw. And then she looked up, and there was her mother!

She was leaning over her, smiling as if the row last night had never happened. She'd promised Gwyn that they'd go up the mountain to their favourite picnic spot. There'd be no jobs about the house – not today. This wasn't an ordinary day. It was Abren's first proper day back home with them – and they were going to spend it celebrating!

Abren sat up in the bed, holding the cutlass ever tighter. The sun was shining, the morning outside her window crystal-clear. All the way down to the forest she could see sunlight and bright colours. It could almost have been a perfect morning – almost have been yesterday, as her mother wanted her to believe, and everything that had happened since a bad dream.

But Abren knew it wasn't just a dream. She didn't need to see the shutters hidden behind the curtains to know that she was a prisoner. Didn't need to see the key in her mother's pocket.

She got up, though, and played along with it, got dressed and even put down the cutlass when her mother told her to. Downstairs she found the knapsack packed with a picnic lunch, just like yesterday. Gwyn smiled when Abren walked in. It was as if she'd never pleaded with him last night, and he'd never turned his face away. As if they'd never fought each other and she hadn't seen the hate. As if they were an ordinary sister and brother.

'We thought we'd make an early start,' he said. 'Let's be off, shall we?'

He slung the knapsack over his shoulder. Abren thought about going back for the cutlass, but it was too late. Her mother stood in the doorway, hands on her hips, calling her out. She smiled as Abren followed her into the yard, and Abren wanted to cry. Gwyn pulled on a pair of big, steel-capped walking boots, and her mother found herself a good stout stick. She thwacked the air with it, and laughed in high old spirits. She stood on one side of Abren, and Gwyn stood on the other. He was smiling fit to burst. They both were. It was an ugly sight.

'Let's be off, then,' Gwyn said.

They started across the yard, Abren shuffling and trying to hang back. More than ever, she felt like a prisoner. She hunched her shoulders, cursed herself for letting the cutlass go, and stuck her bare hands in her pockets. Immediately, she felt something down there. Something heavy and smooth, like a stone.

She pulled it out, hoping that it might serve as a weapon. But it was only the second Miss Ingram's gift of mead, twisted in a slip of paper. Abren sighed with disappointment, and was about to put it back. But her mother saw what she was holding – and her face blanched.

'What have you got there?'

Abren held up the mead, and the sun shone through it. Just a little gift of shining gold to remind her of the mountain, but her mother cried out and tried to grab it. Abren sprang back, clutching the glass tight. *Too tight.* It crushed between her fingers and the mead came oozing out – a sticky sweetness that mingled with her blood.

Her mother saw it, and caught its rich, musky smell. She cried again.

'Look what you've done!'

Abren didn't know what she had done, staring at her hand, sticky with glass and mead and blood. But before she could even find the words to ask – the bees struck.

Suddenly, there they were, pouring over the house as if answering the call of Plynlimon Mountain nectar. Abren stared at them in astonishment, scarcely able to believe that the dark cloud rushing towards her was alive. It passed her by, ignoring her completely and heading for her mother instead. The air was heavy with the sound of bees muttering with anger.

Abren's mother turned and ran. So did Gwyn. But there could be no escaping. The cloud dropped on them, and the last Abren saw was her brother's fists punching the air and her mother's stick making everything worse as it flailed through the cloud, rousing the bees to new heights of fury.

They were St Curig's bees, of course.

Cŵn y Wbir

Abren followed the stream up through the misty forest. Common sense told her to get off the mountain, but a deeper sense by far kept her climbing. There was only one river in her life and she'd got to get to the heart of it. The heart of her story, discovered at last, and the heart of the river, rising on Plynlimon.

Abren scrambled over roots and stones, knowing that her mother and brother would soon come after her and no bees could stop them. The higher she climbed, the stiller and cooler the day became. A little mist appeared between the trees, and the blue sky started disappearing until, by the time that Abren emerged on to the open mountain, the sunny day had completely gone.

Abren pressed on all the same, keeping close to the stream just as the first Miss Ingram had told her. By now, the mist had turned to thick cloud. It was hard to believe that there were hills out there, and valleys rolling on to a distant horizon.

Finally, Abren couldn't even see the stream. It cut down deeply between banks of peat, and all she could do was follow the sound of it. But even that became impossible as the peaty ground all around her started sucking and burbling, whistling and squelching.

Abren realised that she had stumbled into a bog, hidden beneath reeds and mosses. Cobwebs brushed her legs, perfectly shaped as if nobody had ever walked here before. Her feet started sinking and she tried to head for higher ground where a few sheep stood watching her. But at every step she took, the ground gave way beneath her and she sank even further.

In the end she gave up and turned back. She had lost the stream, and it would be crazy to carry on. She looked for the forest, thinking to retrace her steps, but couldn't see a single tree. She headed for where she guessed the forest ought to be, placing every step carefully. But her caution made no difference.

The further she progressed, the worse things got. She sank even further. Plunged on in the hope of finding a foothold, only to find her ankles disappearing. Step by step they sank in deeper, and her balance started going. She looked about for something to grip. But there wasn't as much as a thistle to cling on to!

There wasn't *anything* – and the peat-black water was inching up her legs. She couldn't pull them out. It was all happening so quickly! Abren cried for help – but her voice bounced back at her as if held in by a wall of cloud. She tried another step – and started teetering sideways. Tried to right herself – and landed in the bog!

It wrapped itself around her like a cold embrace. Abren couldn't move, crushed by its weight. She couldn't get up, for all her struggling. Her body was stuck, and her legs were sinking. She tried to lift them, but it was impossible.

She cried again. Suddenly someone came towards her, striding through the mist! She waved and yelled.

'Help me! Help me, help!'

The figure carried on, and she saw it was her brother. *It was Gwyn!* He came towards her across the mountain grassland, and Abren wept with relief. His face and arms were swollen with bee stings, but whatever had been between them belonged in the past. Everything was different now. Nothing would stop her brother rescuing his sister nor her mother either, coming up behind him. Abren cried for help and her mother's face, swollen with bee stings too, crumpled into a smile. And suddenly Abren realised. Suddenly she knew. '*A death by drowning*,' the smile said, and it wasn't her mother's smile, nor were the cold eyes that stared at her predicament her mother's eyes.

They were a false-mother's eyes, belonging to a woman she had never recognised. A women whom she now knew was – Queen Gwendolina.

Abren cried again. There was only one story in her life, with only one conclusion.

She held out her arms, but without hope. The false-mother smiled again and Abren knew that she would die. She whimpered like a baby, and the bog whimpered back at her, sucking and whistling, and pulling her down to a world where mountains and streams and forests were all gone. Where Pengwern was gone, and all her friends and every hope of rescue.

Abren fought and struggled, but it made no difference. She felt herself slipping into the darkness. Felt the bog close over her, its peaty blackness all around her. Felt it push her down like a dead weight, clutching her in an iron embrace which would squeeze the last life out of her.

She braced herself for it. Waited for the end – and

suddenly found herself rising instead of sinking! The bog pulled one way and something pulled the other. What was going on? It was like being on the island again, underneath the railway bridge. Something had got her under the shoulders, and she was rising like a cork drawn from a bottle.

She was bursting free, like a newborn baby. Light greeted her – the dull light of a cloudy mountain top, but for Abren it could have been the brightest sun. The world roared around her and for an exhilarating moment she felt as light as air. Then gravity took over and she found herself flat out on the ground, with hard hands pounding her back to life.

'That's it! Good girl! Breathe, yes – *breathe*!'

Black stuff oozed and spluttered out of Abren's mouth and nose and every pore. She lay in a mass of tangled arms and legs, unable to move except to blink open her eyes. She looked up slowly and there above her was – *the mountain man*.

He looked down at her, his eyes as dark as ever and his silver charms dangling round his neck. His dogs panted over her, and Abren tried to find the words to thank him. He smiled at her, and the expression in his eyes was unfathomable. It could have been anything. Could have been love. Could have been pity. Could even have been hate.

Abren closed her eyes again. All around her she could hear the grey dogs whining and the ground sucking and burbling. She could feel the ground shaking, and when she finally dared look it was Gwendolina, this time, who was stuck in the bog. Gwendolina fighting for her life.

What had happened to bring this about?

Abren watched in horror as the false-mother struggled to get free. The dogs whined again and the mountain man shouted at them to shut up. And at the sound of his voice Abren caught a whiff of something cold and manky coming off Gwendolina. She had never smelt it before, but she knew what it was.

It was fear. The smell of it driving the dogs crazy – and the mountain man had to shout at them again. He rose to his feet, and Gwendolina trembled before him. 'I never meant to cross you! I only meant to put things right! All I wanted was the chance to prove myself!'

'*A chance like that comes at a price!*'

'I owed it to myself.'

'*No, you owe me!*'

The two of them stood locked together. The dogs snapped their teeth, but the mountain man still held them back. Their coats bristled, the red spots on them standing out like wounds. Gwendolina sank back from them into the bog, the smile wiped off her face, never to return. She called for Gwyn, and he came rushing to her aid, fool that he was.

Immediately, he started sinking too. The mountain man watched without expression on his face, but Abren stared in horror as the bog rose around them. A thousand feelings clamoured, starting with revenge and finishing with simple human fellow feeling. She wanted them to sink, and yet she couldn't just stand by. Wanted them to die, but knew she had to do something.

She struggled to her feet – but it was already too late. The false mother toppled forward on her face, followed by Gwyn. He tried to right himself, but only sank in deeper. Abren made to spring towards them, unable to contain herself any longer.

But the mountain man wouldn't let her. He held her back.

'There's nothing we can do!'

At his words, Abren felt herself turn as cold as death. She couldn't believe that the mountain man – who had rescued her – wouldn't do the same for Gwyn and Gwendolina! She tried to tear herself away from him. To rescue them herself. But as if she didn't want Abren's help, Queen Gwendolina screamed at her:

'May you never rest in peace! May you never love! May you never, ever find your true self!'

She screamed the words as if a curse. An age-old curse upon them all, and not just Abren. Upon the king, her husband, who'd betrayed her. Upon the elf-maid, Effrildis, who'd driven her out. Upon their child, Abren, who had stolen her child Gwyn's place in their father's life and in his heart. And upon the mountain man, too, who had turned on her in the moment of her triumph, and snatched it away.

Abren understood. She bowed her head. And the mountain man must have understood too, for suddenly his dogs tore from his side and before the false mother could call down yet more curses, they were upon her, yelping and howling, churning up the bog and calling down a nightmare upon her and her hapless son.

Abren screamed. She'd have hauled the dogs back if she could. But she didn't have the power – and the mountain man wouldn't let her, anyway. He held her tight in his arms. All she could do was watch as a swirling cloud of giant shapes, dark as night and speckled as if with blood, trampled the bog as if it held no fears for them, then rolled across the mountain, melting into the mist, baying as they disappeared.

When silence fell at last, the bog was flat. Nothing of Gwyn remained. Nothing of Gwendolina, except the little piece of string which she had taken off the corph candle. It lay among the reeds on the edge of the bog. The mountain man stooped and picked it up.

'If you play with fire, then it will get you,' he said. 'If you light the corph candle, then the death by drowning you call down could be your own!'

He tucked the string into his pocket. There were no signs on the bog that there had ever been a struggle. Not a mark of pounding dogs.

'What *are* those creatures?' Abren said. Her voice was shaking.

The mountain man looked down at her.

'Those were the *Cŵn y Wbir.*'

The source

Abren clung on to the mountain man. Whatever he had allowed to become of Gwyn and Gwendolina, he was still her rescuer. She was safe from the bog – and it was because of him.

'They'll never bother you again. Never touch you, little Abren,' he said.

Crushed against his chest, Abren felt his heart flutter as he spoke. Who *was* he, she asked herself, who had snatched her from the pit of death, and now held her as if he'd never let go? Who *was* he, calling her 'little Abren', as if she meant something to him? Something special – precious, even.

Abren looked up at the mountain man. Surely she didn't need to ask. She knew already. *It was obvious.* The man who held her in his arms was every inch a king! Every inch a figure out of legend, with clouds swirling around him and his black eyes just like hers!

'You're the king of Pengwern, aren't you?' Abren, scarcely dared to speak the words. '*You're my father!*'

She looked up. Here was what she'd looked for all along – the heart of her story, at long last, and *her own flesh and blood.* She held her breath, waiting for acknowledgment to write itself upon the mountain man's face.

But instead he threw back his head and laughed. And when Abren looked into his eyes, there wasn't any humour in them. Wasn't the 'welcome home' that she had hoped for, or a father's recognition.

Abren knew that she'd made a terrible mistake. This man wasn't her father, after all! His heart might beat like flesh and blood, fluttering at the mention of her name, and he might even look like her, with the same black eyes – but he was just a stranger. And not just any stranger, either! *What had she been thinking of?* This man was a murderer! She'd seen what he'd allowed to happen to Gwyn and Gwendolina. And now here he was, holding her in his arms as if she were his prisoner!

Abren tried to tear herself away, but the mountain man held on.

'Not so fast, little Abren,' he said in a cold, tight voice which Abren knew she'd never forget.

She struggled like a bird caught in a trap.

'What are you doing? What's the matter with you? *Let me go!*'

She kicked and fought, but it made no difference – the mountain man held her tighter than ever.

'I want to show you something,' he said. 'Something that you've searched for and would give anything to see. And here it is, at long last. Call it a gift, if you like. A farewell gift from me. Look here, *in my eyes ...*'

The last thing Abren wanted was to look again into the mountain man's eyes. She tried to turn her face away, but it was impossible to avoid his gaze. It bore down into her and everything else seemed to fade. No longer were the eyes black, but silver like a mirror. And there was a world in that silver light, shining as if reflected. In it, crows wheeled through the sky. And trees swayed on a hill, with a river running round it.

And a palace stood upon the hill. A pure white palace. Abren recognised its high white walls, built to keep out every danger. Recognised its gateways and its towers.

It was her home.

Abren cried out, staring into the mountain man's eyes, and reaching for a world which wasn't just reflected, but real. Real enough to touch and real enough to visit, passing smoking hearths with maids and soldiers clustered round them. Sweeping up staircases. Peering into room after room. Reaching one room in particular, and peeping like a little, playful child round the door. And there, at a window, a woman sat stitching, her needle catching the sun.

Abren saw it flashing – *and remembered*. She remembered the room, and she remembered the woman's hair falling over her face, casting it in shadows. She didn't need to see the face to know. *This was her mother's room!* Her mother's, and hers too! The one where she'd been born and had grown up as a child. The one where she'd lived happy days, and slept at night in a narrow bed. The one where she had sat at her mother's feet, jumbling her skeins of thread, copying her fairy stitches, sharing the moment when she'd finished her embroidery and held it up, smiling and crying out, 'There! At last! What do you think? *It's for you ...*'

And *it* was Abren's little blanket! Her comfort blanket which her mother had given her, sliding it around Abren's shoulders and knotting it under her chin. Abren remembered the moment as if it had only been yesterday. Remembered being a child in this room. Not a child in a homework poem, or the heroine in a legend which had grown around her life. But the real her. Abren. Here she was, at last. She could see herself.

And she could see her mother, too, looking down at her with the litttle blanket round her shoulder. And surely this was the moment which she had waited for ever since the night mists parted and she had floated through – a body on a river without a memory or name.

Abren raised her face to meet her mother's gaze.

'Enough of that! *The peep-show's over!*'

The mountain man blinked – and it was all gone. Abren came to herself upon a lonely mountain top. There was no palace made of white stone. No room with narrow bed and stone floor. No mother looking down at her, ready to receive her daughter's gaze.

'Please,' Abren whispered. 'Not yet, please! *Bring her back!*'

The mountain man looked away. He didn't answer. Didn't curse at her, like Gwendolina. Didn't shout at her, nor waste his time on a final speech which explained who he was and why she deserved his hate. He just picked her up and marched out into the bog.

'The river may have helped you once, long ago,' he said. 'It may have saved you from that poor fool Gwendolina! But it won't help you this time! It won't dare. If you want a thing done, you have to do it yourself! You're not her kill this time – *you're mine!*'

Peaty water splashed around them, but the mountain man strode through it as if the bog couldn't touch him. Abren beat his chest, slapped his face and tugged his hair. But it was a pitiful little battle, lost before it ever started. The mountain man strode on until there was nothing but bog on every side of them – an unrelenting view, with not a tree or bush or rock in sight.

At last he stopped. Clouds swirled around them, and he looked down at Abren with a grudging hint of cold pity. Abren stopped hitting him, and clung on for dear life.

'Please, oh, please, *oh*, *please!*' she said.

It made no difference. There was no reasoning with the mountain man. He prised her helpless little body off him, and laid it down in the bog! Laid it like a baby being tucked up for the night – then turned away like a cruel father, leaving his child without a light, even though he knew she feared the dark. Then he walked away without looking back.

Abren watched him go. And when the bog rolled over her, she didn't fight. What was the point? It wasn't Gwendolina she was up against this time. It was this man who owned the mountain, with its storms and bogs and clouds, its forests and its streams. Who owned everything that moved upon Plynlimon.

And now he owned Abren too.

She closed her eyes. The bog slipped round her shoulders and under her chin, like a cold blanket of death. It oozed into her mouth, however tightly she tried to keep it shut, and filled her nose. It filled her ears and soaked through her skin, found her veins and infused them with black poison, clogged her arteries and flooded into her lungs.

So this was how her story ended, after all her struggles to make sense of things! Underneath the mountain in the dark; far from Pengwern and her friends; far from the river whose source she'd never found: far from that room where she had been a happy child, and far from her mother.

Abren sank down and down. A kaleidoscope of fleeting memories jumbled up together until only blackness remained. It filled her and she couldn't feel, breathe, think, speak. Couldn't find that will to live which had stopped her story ending on chapter one. Couldn't cry out, as she had done then, for, *'Just a chance – that's all I ask.'*

Now her chances were all spent. She free-fell through the darkness, wanting nothing but oblivion – short and sharp and *let's get on with it*. But somewhere underneath her, Abren heard something. Heard it as she'd heard it before, under the railway bridge, and in Bentley's living room at Christmas, and on the willow island only last night. And it wasn't oblivion that waited for her, after all.

It was 'her tune'!

It bubbled up, as sweet as candy and as fresh as air. The tune that said that she was *just fine*. That she was brave and strong and where she should be. That there was nothing to be frightened of. And Abren hadn't lost the river, after all.

She had found its source!

She felt it underneath her, buried deep but rising all the time, bubbling up as fresh as air. And its tune grew as it rose. And the words it sang were, *'TRUST ME'.*

And Abren did! She let the river take her, as it had taken her once long before. The mountain man was wrong to say it wouldn't dare. She felt the clear, fresh water of the Sabrina Fludde soaking through her pores, flushing through her lungs, chasing through her veins. Felt it racing through her heart and freeing it to beat again. *She was alive.* No black corph candle, summoned forth by Gwendolina, could stand in her way! No howling Cyn Ybir – and no mountain man!

Nothing could stand in Abren's way! The river flowed into her and she flowed into it, merging together until no longer could she say 'this is me' or 'this is it'. Her limbs turned into flowing water. Her child's body turned into flowing water. Her face turned into flowing water – eyes, ears, mouth, nose, cheeks, chin and even her hair.

Suddenly she found herself moving and breathing with the river's secret rhythms and its life. Flowing as it flowed, underneath the mountain where nobody could see. A river on a hidden journey underneath the bog – and Abren travelled with it and not even the mountain man could see.

She ran beneath the open grassland, ran beneath grazing sheep, ran deep down beneath banks of peat until the stream broke out into the light; until the mountain top was behind her, and the forest greeted her. Then she ran over its rocks and roots, through its pools and out again, down deep, fast gulleys to the waterfall above Blaen Hafren.

Here, water within water, she tumbled past the house and down the glen, flowing fast and never looking back. Past the quarry she flowed, and under the road. Back into the forest, and down through Old Hall. And once she would have changed lives with those schoolchildren, wending their way home at the end of the day. But now she wouldn't be anyone but Abren, travelling with the stream, and giving it her name.

On she flowed, past St Curig's House, where she looked for the Misses Ingram but couldn't find them, out of Old Hall and down the valley. She flowed past the willow island where Gwyn had found her, and carried on until she couldn't see the great bulk of Plynlimon any more. It lay lost amid its forests, swathed in clouds. Suddenly, Abren was free of it.

At last. She felt herself stop rushing in a panic, and began to flow more gently. With quiet dignity the stream carried her through the little town with the railway station and on into a wider world, where if anyone noticed anything, it wouldn't be a body on the water. It would be a silver river threading home.

The moon was high, and the day was over, at long last. The stream flowed through the darkness, and Abren flowed with it, knowing that nothing could frighten her any more. She laughed as she flowed, and the stream laughed too, drawing new streams to itself and growing into a river big enough to shape a landscape. Hills here, valleys there, towns here, roads there. No one could fight a river which could shape a land like this! Not even the mountain man.

Abren laughed again, flowing on and on as if child and river, day and night, past and present, were one and the same thing. And all that lay behind her was forgotten, and all that lay ahead was – *Pengwern*.

Abren moved towards it like a conqueror returning home. She imagined its towers and spires waiting for her up ahead. Imagined Pen and Sir Henry, Phaze II and Bentley, Fee and Mena – her friends, all ready to forgive her for the things she hadn't told them yet.

But soon she would! Oh, how she would!

Abren laughed again, imagining the cosy fire in Bentley's living room, and all of them gathered round while she told her story.

And suddenly someone laughed back.

The laugh was cold – and Abren froze. She knew who it was, of course. How could she not? She could almost see his eyes, tightening like lenses in his head. See him smiling because he'd found her. What a fool she'd been! She'd thought that she had won. But the battle wasn't even half begun!

Abren took a last glance at the river, as she always wanted to remember it. Then the wind got up, and the moon disappeared. The stars went out, and the mountain man's laughter ran down the water like an electric shock.

Abren felt it strike her, and cried in pain. She had felt his pity, cold and cruel. She had felt his hate.

And now she felt the mountain man's power.

Part Six
River in Flood

Able-bodied men

Rain fell in sheets from a low-flying sky. It hailed down like bullets, riddling the roofs and spires of Pengwern and emptying the streets. It emptied the Quarry Park and left the town centre deserted. Saturday midday – the busiest time of the week – saw scarcely a shopper struggling up Pride Hill against the torrent pouring down from its drains and gulleys. Even the indoor shopping mall was nearly empty, and the market hall was no better, all its stalls set up but nobody in to buy anything.

It wasn't just the storm. People were afraid of coming into town for fear of what the river might do. There had been floods before in Pengwern, but nobody had ever seen the river like this. They stayed indoors, grumbling about the weather report not warning them of trouble, the water authority not 'doing anything' about the water levels, and the town council not getting out the duckboards.

'Just look at it!' they grumbled to each other. 'Look at all that water on the roads! And those cellars flooding! And those drains rising, all over town! This is meant to be the twenty-first century! What's the modern world coming to? Why can't somebody control a little river?'

It was a good question. One which even Bentley asked as he splashed through the rain, delivering a package to one of his mother's customers. Beneath the high town walls, he could see the river swirling like a thick brown stew. Usually it flowed on its way, looking so tame, but now it flooded over pavements and crept up people's gardens, heading for their front doors and sweeping away everything in its path.

There was nothing anyone could do. Bentley shivered with excitement. He reached the customer's house and rang the bell. When there was no reply, he left the package round the back and hurried off to the town walls. Here a small crowd had gathered to take photographs, snapping away undeterred by the rain.

'How could the river rise so fast in just a few hours?' they wanted to know. 'Where's it come from?' 'What's going on?' 'How high is it going to get?'

Bentley glanced up at the sky, its clouds still low and no end in sight. A raw wind blew into his face and howled off along the walls. Briefly, Bentley thought that he could hear the baying of dogs in it. So did everybody else, crying, *What was that?* and looking about.

Bentley didn't wait to find out. He headed for home. The dogs could have been a trick of the storm. But they could have been something else. There was something strange going on. Something *different* about this storm.

It was a relief to get home and slam the front door behind him.

'Is that you, Bentley?' his mum called, concern in her voice, as if she'd regretted sending him out. 'Are you all right?'

Bentley went up to the bathroom for a towel, then came down to the living-room where everything was snug and warm. A fire burned in the grate, and lamps and candles had been lit because the electricity was off. Bentley felt safe from the storm. He assured his mother that he'd delivered the package right into her customer's hands, then sat down to dry himself by the fire.

As he did so, he caught sight of Abren's postcard sitting on the mantelpiece. He picked it up, suddenly missing her again. Turned it over and read her message about being fine. He hoped that she was. The word round town was that the child found under the railway bridge had gone back to her family. He hoped that child was Abren, for her own sake at least.

His father came in, and Bentley asked him if he'd heard any news of Abren. But the only news his dad had heard was of the Welsh Bridge being cut off, the wild west end in trouble and every able-bodied man being needed to fight the flood. He dashed out again into the stormy night, bright-eyed and excited. Bentley's question was left hanging in the air.

'There are things that they can do for us – these able-bodied men!' sniffed Mum. 'And there are things that they pretend to do – like delivering packages, for example, right into a customer's hands. And there are things that they can do nothing about. And fighting floods is one of them! *Nobody can stop the path of a flood!*'

She went up to bed with a candle and a book for company. Bentley was left to marvel at the things his mother knew, no matter how he tried to hide them. He followed later, getting into bed with a candle and a book too, promising himself to listen out for Dad. But he fell asleep almost straight away, and didn't hear a thing until a gust of wind struck the roof, sending tiles crashing down into Dogpole Alley.

Bentley awoke in a panic. The candle had burned down, and in the darkness he heard someone laughing. At first he thought it was someone in the house. But then he realised it was outside, caught up in the wind, like that baying of the dogs. And there was triumph in the laughter. There was something cruel.

Bentley leapt out of bed, his heart thundering. He flung on his clothes, went to look for his dad and, when he saw he wasn't back, went out to find him. What had he been thinking of, lying in bed when the town needed every able-bodied man, woman and child, to fight this terrible storm which had come upon them all?

Bentley left the house and tore across the alley, starting down the Seventy Steps towards the bus station and the wild west end. But at step number fifty-two, counting from the top, he met the river. It stretched out from the step, across the main road, over the bus station, past the houses and pubs around the railway station and out of sight.

Bentley stared at it, shining darkly in the searchlight of a circling helicopter. He had never seen his town like this before. It was a terrifying sight. No army of able-bodied men, women, girls, boys, experts, volunteers, emergency services and circling TV camera crews could possibly make any difference. And the rain was still pouring.

And it was going to get worse.

Abren in flood

Abren swept downriver on a white-knuckle ride. Rain beat upon her as it had done for half the night and all day long, pouring from the sky as if its stopcocks had been left full on. All around her, the river was breaking its banks, bursting everywhere and spilling across the land. And Abren flowed with it, water within water. She was unable to stop herself.

She crashed over river paths and swirled through woods and meadows, running towards Pengwern on a river which was being punished for daring yet again to help Abren. It was as if its wells were being emptied, deep under the mountain, its hidden reservoirs banished, never to return.

And half the land was washing down with it – peaty glens and trees torn from their roots, stone walls and dead sheep. The flood took everything, pouring over roads, cutting off river loops and turning them into lakes, running after animals, and swirling through houses, whose shocked inhabitants were forced to flee.

And Abren ran with it. She had felt the river's rhythms, and felt its life. And now she felt its death. Logs as fast as crocodiles crashed into her like guided missiles, programmed to seek and destroy. Waves ran over her like cold knives. Rain beat down on her like a pitiless jungle drum, and Abren rushed on, taking the fastest ride of all, in the middle of the river where the flood was at its wildest, heading for Pengwern as if it were her only hope.

Finally, the water tower which marked the town's approach appeared against the stormy skyline. Abren rushed towards it, weak with relief. Ahead lay her home, and her only hope of safety. If she could reach those old town walls, they would would wrap themselves around her. Fortress walls of old, they would hold her like a mother, and keep her safe. No flood could rise up that hill where her father's palace had once stood! No mountain man could reach her if only she could get to it!

So Abren plunged towards the town, breaking over jetties, flooding boat sheds, rising up into gardens and reaching houses that stood high above the usual flood plain. She poured into basements and out again, under back doors and through front ones, into car parks and out again until the town was right upon her.

She had reached it at last! She flooded through the loading bays of the new shopping mall, against the Seventy Steps and on into the wild west end where she slapped against the doors of the market hall. The self-same doors where once she'd stared at her reflection, not knowing who she was. And here she was again, knocking on its doors, looking for dry land!

Abren flowed on down the street. All around her, it was getting dark – night-dark as well as storm-dark. There were no lights to brighten the gloom, and Abren saw that she was in the midst of a vast, black lake, with shops and old town mansions rising up like islands. Only the high town remained dry.

Dry and unreachable! Abren rolled towards it, but a council lorry drove her back, dumping sandbags in her path and forcing her towards the main flow of the river. She whirled away, watching dry land disappearing. The river carried her under the Welsh Bridge and past a row of submerged night clubs, along a tree-lined path and into the Quarry Park, its sloping lawns turned into another vast lake.

For all Abren's longing to return to town, she never would have wanted it like this! She flooded over flowerbeds which had once been the town's pride and joy, and along avenues where cyclists once had ridden and families strolled. She washed across the bandstand, sent great statues toppling, reached the school shed which had once given her shelter, crashing against it and breaking it to pieces.

Then she swept on to the quiet haven of Compass House, which was quiet no more, its jetties swept away and its boat shed lying under siege. Its terraced garden lay under water and lights were on all over the house, as if Pen and Sir Henry had realised, though they lived up high above the water, that they were in danger as much as anybody else.

Abren would have stopped to help them if she only could. But the waves drove her on, and the wind beat down on her, fiercer than ever. And in it she could have sworn she heard the howl of the Cŵn y Wbir.

She shuddered and hurried on, telling herself that she had imagined it. Ahead of her stood the English Bridge, its stone arches all but submerged. She swept beneath them with only inches to spare – and suddenly, there in front of her, was the last bridge of all.

The railway bridge.

It sat in the shadow of the castle, on the wildest

stretch of river, taking the full brunt of the flood. And the first time Abren had seen it she'd thought it was a monster. But now she knew it was a friend. She knew it was all that stood between her and the mountain man. It was her last chance to save herself.

Abren dashed towards the bridge, past a scene of devastation. Gone were the football pitch and the car parks next to it, and the roads out of town. Gone, too, were the houses behind the pitch – rows upon rows of them had disappeared into the dark flood waters.

Abren could have wept for all those people with their ruined homes. But she dashed on, water within water, unable to do anything else. The railway bridge drew close, and whirlpools slapped their way beneath it. Black waves broke over the girders in sheets of white foam, and Abren rode the waves as the bridge loomed overhead. If she was going to save herself, she had to do it now, out in the middle of the flood, where the waters were at their fastest and the waves at their highest.

She reared up with them, reaching for the bridge. First time she wasn't high enough, but second time the waves broke over an iron walkway where she had once run, and sat, and played. And she broke with them. And when the waves fell back, the little bit of water that was Abren remained. The flood flowed on, and a little pool of water lay on the girder, quietly unnoticed.

She had done it! *She was safe.*

Exhaustion overwhelmed Abren. She had been crushed, but not broken, battered and pulled, thrust and hurled. She had been turned into water, and now as water she lay – a little pool of stillness, taking her deserved rest.

And the rest was sweet. No mountain man could see her with his black eyes which saw everything. Not here, under the dark railway bridge. No Cŵn y Wbir could call her, and her rest was silent.

When she awoke again, *she was herself*.

She felt her arms and legs and body, felt her eyes and mouth, her nose and chin. Felt her wet hair dripping down her face. No longer was she water within water. She was Abren again.

She laughed out loud, looking at the railway bridge, and knowing that she'd come home. Somewhere nearby was her father's palace, and somewhere, too, were memories of better days. Not nightmare memories, stalking her through streets. But memories of a life that any child would want to live. And Abren wanted it again. She wanted to play with skeins of thread at her mother's feet. *Wanted to see her mother's face.*

Abren scrambled to her feet. She had no idea how she was supposed to find her mother, after all this time. But as if there were no flood rising under her, seeking to destroy the town and flush her out, she started making her way along the girders. She jumped the jump, slipped through the darkness of the black stone arches and finally ended up in Phaze II's room, stripped bare, just as she'd left it.

What was she going to do now? She looked down the room, and the door to Old Sabrina's room stood open. A little light came seeping through it and Abren knew for sure that Old Sabrina was still there. She was in that room, holding her life together against vandals and floods. And she mightn't be Gwendolina, as Abren had once thought, but there was only one story in Abren's life, and whoever the old woman really was – *she had a part to play.*

Croydon Central Library

Tel: 020 3700 1034 or 1038

Borrowed Items 09/09/2019 13:30

XXXXXXXXX7707

Item Title	Due Date
* The trophy child	30/09/2019

Amount Outstanding: £6.00

* Indicates items borrowed today
Thank you for using self-service
www.croydonlibraries.com

Effrildis

Old Sabrina sat as if she hadn't moved for weeks. A spider ran across her face on a cobweb track between her cardigan and bird's-nest hair. Her plate of food lay mouldy on the floor, and her feet rested in a pile of ash, blown down the chimney.

Ash covered everything, from the old woman to the piano, and from the chandelier to the mirror in which she sat reflected without moving. Was she alive or was she dead? It was hard to tell.

Abren took a closer look – and lying in the old woman's lap she saw her little comfort blanket. Her blanket, which she'd thought she'd lost! She let out a cry, and Old Sabrina finally noticed that she had company. She twisted her head and looked up at Abren for the first time. Abren felt herself turn cold inside. There was something hidden in the old woman's face. Something underneath the ash and grime. *But what was it?*

'I d– didn't mean to startle you,' she said. 'It's just that you've got my –'

She broke off. Old Sabrina was staring at her, clutching the blanket tight, as if she'd never let go. Her mouth was moving up and down, but nothing was coming out. Her face was peering up through the shadows of her bird's-nest hair. And *Abren had seen that face before.*

'No! *Never! It isn't possible! IT CAN'T BE ...!*'

Rain came bursting through the ceiling – a sharp reminder that the flood was out there, and still rising. But Abren never saw it. All she saw was Old Sabrina's face, staring at her as she'd never stared before. And it looked so tired, that sad old face. It looked so cold and bitter. It was impossible to imagine that it had ever been different from what it was now. And Old Sabrina's hands, too, clutching the blanket. It was impossible to imagine stiff old fingers like these ever holding a needle, or embroidering fairy stitches, or fastening off with a flourish, crying, 'There, it's finished!' with a smile as she spoke.

Impossible to imagine this half-dead old woman ever smiling at all, or being beautiful enough to win a king, or loving him, or giving birth to a child, or calling that child ...

Abren turned away with a small gasp. This was it – the moment that she'd waited for above all others! The one she'd pleaded with the mountain man to let her see. *And yet it couldn't be.* It wasn't fair!

Not her! she thought. Not a terrible old woman like that! Why can't she be somebody like the Misses Ingram with their honey cakes and amber tea? Why can't I go home to a garden full of bees and yew trees? *Why can't my mother be the one I want her to be?*

There was no answer to Abren's question. Nor could there ever be. But suddenly, as if the old woman had heard it and wanted to set the record straight, she struggled to her swollen feet. Abren rushed to help, but she wouldn't have it. Maybe she was too proud. Maybe Abren had hurt her with her silent indignation. But straightening herself up, she leant across and slid the blanket round Abren's shoulders, pulling it straight and tying it under her chin. Her fingers fumbled over the knot, and her eyes were full of pain. But she smiled, all the same. Smiled as if to say, 'You were wrong. I can do it! I can smile. *See?*'

And Abren saw. How could she not? The face that smiled at her was her mother's!

At long last.

'I thought I'd never find you,' Abren said, as if in a dream. 'Thought I didn't stand a chance. And now here you are, and the things I tried to find were here all along, hidden underneath the railway bridge. No wonder the river always brought me back to it!'

Old Sabrina eased herself back into her chair, as if the pain of standing were more than she could bear. Yet more rain poured through the ceiling, bringing plaster with it – and she seemed to notice at last.

'I think that we've been found,' she whispered in a low voice, which wasn't used to speaking. 'Finally flushed out. This always was a safe place. So dark and quiet. But now I think he knows where we are.'

Abren felt herself turn cold all over. 'The mountain man? *You know him?*' she said.

Old Sabrina looked at her. The sadness in her eyes could have filled a lake.

'Who told Gwendolina where to find you, all those years ago?' she whispered in a croaky little voice. 'Who told her all about you in the first place – seeing my little struggles to be happy and playing us both like pawns in his game? *Of course I know who he is!*'

'Tell me!' Abren cried out. 'I want to know. *And tell me why he hates me so much?*'

Old Sabrina lowered her eyes. For a moment she couldn't speak, then, 'It's all because of me,' she said.

'Because of what I did to him. It's me he's out to get, not you. He'll punish you to get at me. He'll even destroy Pengwern if he thinks that it will hurt me. He's my father, you see!'

'He's your ...?'

'He's your grandfather.'

Another piece of plaster came crashing from the ceiling, but Abren never saw it. Instead, she saw the mountain man's eyes, which were black like hers, and felt the way his heart had fluttered when he'd called her 'little Abren'.

'It can't be!' she cried out. But in the cold places deep inside herself, it all rang true.

'He always swore he'd get me,' Old Sabrina said. 'I was his elf-child. That's what he called me. His baby daughter, born on the mountain when it was young. When its rivers were like sisters, and we played together like best friends. And the mountain was my inheritance, and I turned my back on it. I gave it up – *for love.'*

There was something dreadful about the way the old woman said the word *love*.

More of the ceiling crashed down, and water came seeping through from Phaze II's room. The flood had reached the railway bridge, rising through its chasms. But neither of them noticed.

'The king of Pengwern said I was his love,' Old Sabrina said, remembering back. 'He wooed me with false promises. He was your father, and he promised me you'd be his heir. I never knew about his son, who you'd displaced. Never knew about his queen, cast out on my account, cursing me and plotting her revenge. All the sorrow I've endured, all the pain and suffering,

214

all the life we never lived together, you and I – it's him I blame. And I blame him, too, for what he brought out of your grandfather. Things I never knew were there. He wasn't always what you see now – *and neither was I!* This is what he's made me! Not Effrildis any more, giving up my mountain in the name of love. But Old Sabrina, full of hate!'

Hate again. Abren shivered, remembering the Misses Ingram's warning about something brewing on the mountain. It had been hate then, hadn't it, and now it was just the same. Dark, old, cruel hate, as if they'd all been cursed by Gwendolina never to forgive, and never love. So *this* was where the story ended – in this flood where the only king was hate.

Abren looked into her mother's face. 'What happened to my father?' she said, seeing secrets in it, prisoners to the hate. 'The king of Pengwern? What became of him? You know, don't you? He's here somewhere, isn't he – still alive, like you and me? Don't tell me he's not, because I won't believe you. You've got him somewhere, haven't you? *You've done something to him.*'

Old Sabrina didn't answer, but her face said it all. Suddenly, it was her father's face, right down to his remorseless black eyes. And Abren knew why the river had brought her back to Pengwern. It wasn't just to find herself and the answers to her questions. It wasn't even to find her mother. *It was to end the hate.*

She hauled Old Sabrina out of her chair, regardless of swollen feet, and dragged her across the floor to the mirror.

'Take a look!' she cried. 'See what I see when I look at you! See what hate has done! You could have fought it, but you fed it instead! Could have fought Gwendolina's curse, but you chose to live with it! So don't blame love for what you are. Don't blame anyone. *You did it to yourself!*'

The old woman stared at her wrinkle lines as deep as knife wounds, eyes as black as bogs, and bitter mouth. By now half the ceiling was down, and the chandelier with it. Rain scoured the room, driven by the storm, and yet more water came through the door.

'Whatever happened in the past is over!' Abren said. 'The flood's rising and we've got to stop it. Stop it in its tracks and end the hate. Break the power of the mountain man. And only we can do it! The two of us together. Abren and Effrildis. And if we don't, not only we but *the whole town will be lost!*'

Old Sabrina stared at Abren in the mirror. She didn't want to break the power of anything. You could see it in the way she held her head. Didn't want to be Effrildis. Just wanted to be left alone.

But she *was* Effrildis. Despite everything.

'Find your precious father, if you must, and bring him here. I'll never forget – so don't ask me that. I'll never love him like I did. But I'll try my best to forgive.'

She turned her face away. Abren sighed, but her relief was short-lived.

'I don't know where to look,' she said.

'He's where he always has been, all alone,' her mother said. 'A king in his own kingdom. Where I left him on the day when you were snatched. In his palace. *The Palace of Pengwern.*'

The Palace of Pengwern

Abren left the waiting room the way she'd done it before – through a boarded window. She dropped to the rusty railway track, squeezed between the Guinness hoardings and climbed on to the old abandoned platform.

Here the railway lines no longer snaked their way out of town, but disappeared beneath the flood. The view was unforgettable, lit by a single helicopter searchlight, circling overhead. The river had risen level with the top of the railway bridge, and covered everything in sight, except the station platforms and a single signal box.

But Abren didn't have the time to stop and marvel. She made her getaway while she could, hoping against all hope that Old Sabrina would be safe, standing against the flood. She ran down the platform and through the gate at the end. Here the path was dry, but the station forecourt underneath it lay beneath metres of water. The roads around the station were flooded too, and so were the pubs and shops. Only the high town remained dry – if *dry* were the right word for it!

Abren hurried along the path up the hill, battling against overflowing gutters, bursting drains and water gushing out of broken basement windows. Streams poured down the road, and the town was dark without its streetlights.

But it made no difference whether Abren could see or not. She didn't know where she was going. Didn't have a clue where her father's palace might be in this modern town. Didn't even know how she'd recognise her father when she found him.

She tried to imagine him, tall and stately, with a kindly smile and looking like a king. Tried to trust her memory. But as she had discovered, memories were strange things – they didn't always turn up what you expected!

Abren did her best all the same, searching through the rain for palaces and kings. People passed her by, but none of them were likely candidates – figures stooped beneath the rain, crying to each other about the highest flood in recorded memory, and how they'd always remember it. They thought it was exciting – one of those occasions like millennium night, which they'd tell the grandchildren about in years to come. They didn't realise what danger they were in.

Abren hurried past them, knowing only too well! Rain blew into her face like a hail of arrows. It stung her skin and the cold wind tried to force her back. But she pressed on all the same, looking everywhere for a bit of old wall, a window or a gateway that would bring back memories. She passed the old library with its ancient porch and columns carved in stone, passed the half-timbered houses on the hill, reached the castle gate, and stood under its old arch, sheltering from the rain.

But here, yet again, was nothing that she recognised.

She turned to carry on. But suddenly she saw a little tower built into the far side of the castle wall. It was covered in scaffolding, and was in a state of disrepair. A crumbling staircase wound up its side, cordoned off with a sign which read, DANGER. FALLING MASONRY. KEEP OUT!

At the sight of it, not even falling masonry could have kept Abren out. She ran across the castle's inner courtyard, slipped under the cord and bounded up the steps, two at a time. Surely here in this old tower, which had withstood armies and the ravages of time, her father would be waiting! She reached the top and rushed across the flat roof, sure that she would find him. But nobody waited for her. The roof was empty, save for a flagpole flapping in the wind.

Abren struggled to stand upright. Tears pricked her eyes with disappointment. She turned to go, and a helicopter arched overhead. Its searchlight passed over the flood, and in it Abren saw the floating shapes of bikes and cars, bits of furniture, children's toys, old doors, bales of hay, trees torn from their roots and boats torn from their moorings. She even saw a dead dog, caught in the circle of light, and a couple of dead cattle.

Precious lives – and all lost! Precious belongings which had had their places in memory and affection! *And all of them swept away!*

Abren knew that she had to find her father – and quickly, too, before the whole town was destroyed. She turned to climb down from the tower, and something caught her eye, lit up by the helicopter. There it stood in the highest part of town, safe above the flood waters and surrounded by trees.

The ruined outline of Old St Chad's church.

Crows were sitting on it – dark shapes crouched like

silent witnesses, black as mourners in their soaking feathers. And suddenly it was all just like the poem had said – the one for which the schoolboy had got a big 'well done'. The legend of Sabrina Fludde, complete with weeping walls. And they were weeping still – weeping with the rain!

Abren looked at them – *and remembered them* ...

She left the tower, as if no wind and rain could ever hold her back, tearing out of the castle and through the town, past lanes where once she'd skipped and played – and now she could remember them! She tore past the high town cross, where they used to hang men in her father's day. Tore down Pride Hill, where the hawkers used to sell their wares and buskers played. Tore through Dogpole Alley and into Old St Chad's Square.

And here she didn't need the schoolboy's poem to tell her that she had come home!

She stopped running at last. Looked at the old church on its grassy mound, and saw, beneath its crow-lined walls, the once white stones of a great hall. Saw smoking fires, and people clustered round them. Saw sweeping staircases, and rooms hanging with tapestries. Saw one room in particular, and it was her room, with her narrow bed in it, and her mother stitching at the window.

Everything she saw was here somewhere, buried under centuries of other buildings, other lives, generation after generation. And now only the tallest walls remained, built into a church which – in its turn – had become a ruin.

Abren saw it all at last. And she saw the moment

when her happiness was snatched away. It had happened right here in this square! She should have realised when that awful woman turned upon the child. But the memory had been too powerful – and she hadn't dared.

Abren crossed the square. She knew what she was here for, and she knew where to look. She reached the mound and started round it, trusting to her memory. Found the iron-grilled gate and slipped through into a darkness which was cold and wet – full of water, just like all the basements across the town.

But it didn't deter Abren – and neither did the knowledge that something nasty had once scared her down here. She *had* to do this, for her mother's sake, and for her own, and for the town. She edged into the darkness, waist-deep in icy water.

'*Father,*' she whispered. 'Father ... Dad ... Daddy ... Your Majesty ... this is me, Abren, calling you. *Do you hear me?*'

There was no reply, save for slapping water against a far wall. Abren waded on – and tried again in a louder voice.

'*Father!* You must be here somewhere! I know you are! *Answer me!*'

Still no one answered. All Abren heard was her own voice echoing in the darkness. She tried again, shouting this time.

'*KING OF PENGWERN – DO YOU HEAR ME?*'

Again there was no reply. Abren struck a wall, not realising how close it was, and bloodied her face. She leant against it, weeping with frustration and shivering with a cold that started deep down inside and had nothing to do with flood waters. Finally, she started to

221

feel her way along the wall again, muttering and whimpering, but this time not expecting a reply.

'Father, oh, father, oh, please! Mother's waiting ... Effrildis, that is ... Wants to make amends ... make peace, put things right! Get you to her ... flood waters rising ... break the curse! End the hate, or we'll all drown!'

This last was clearer than the rest – and likely to happen sooner than Abren had expected! Water suddenly came pouring through the iron-grilled gate from the road outside. Abren turned at the sound of it, and gasped in horror at the realisation that the flood had reached even Old St Chad's Square, at the top of the town. She turned to get out as quickly as she could, and touched something in her panic. Touched something *clammy*, as she had touched it once before.

Abren screamed. She tried to get away and dimly made out something crouched high on the wall. The smell wafting down from it was overwhelming. It came from rotten clothes, hanging in rags. Bursting boots and filthy feet. Matted hair and a stinking beard. Parchment-yellow, long teeth, and glazed eyes shining almost white as they looked down upon Abren.

Her hands flew to her face, and her heart rattled like a drum roll. She had found a mother turned old by hate. And now, perched on a ledge above the flood, she'd found a father, too. She knew she had. *And what a father!* Not the one she'd hoped for, tall and stately, with a kindly smile and looking like a king. But the man her mother had loved. And Abren must have loved him too, because she was his daughter. And she'd hoped to recognise him when she saw him. And she did.

He was the Chadman.

Part Seven
Queen of Rivers

A pinch of dust

Abren emerged into the square to find people at windows, standing behind their curtains witnessing a drama which affected all their lives. The flood had reached them at last! It flowed round the square, surged through their gates, dashed up their garden paths and battered their front doors.

Abren knew it was too late to get back to the railway station. She looked around in desperation – and there stood Bentley on the grassy mound. Bentley – who had been out, like half the town, to marvel at what was going on. And now here he was, stranded just a few steps from his home, staring wide-eyed as if Abren were the last person he expected to see!

She scrambled up to join him, dragging the Chadman after her, staring round at his deluged square as if he couldn't believe what had happened to it. The rain poured down and the wind lashed into them, but he scuttled into the shelter of his ruined palace walls as if he didn't care about anyone but himself. He was no king standing up for his subjects, no father offering his daughter protection. He didn't call Abren by her name, nor turn to make sure that she was all right, nor offer her the benefits of age and wisdom. He was like a little old lost child, whimpering against the wall, desperate to go home.

Not that there was any home to go to – not any more! Abren looked past Bentley to the faces at the windows. *Scuds*, Phaze II had called them. *Stupid scuds*. And the flood would get them, too. They could climb up to their attics, climb the trees which grew on the mound, climb the highest town walls. But nothing in this town was beyond the reach of the rising waters. It would get Bentley, who watched the waters inching closer all the time. And it would get the Chadman too – poor old, shambling man who'd helped himself to one too many wives, but didn't deserve a fate like this! The flood would destroy them all. And it wasn't fair. It wasn't their battle – *it was hers*.

Abren looked about her in despair. Where was the Misses Ingram's amber mead, shining with a light which summoned armies of bees? Where was the river, which had been Abren's rescuer? Where was anything that might come to their defence, from Sir Henry Morgan's cutlass to Effrildis's elven wisdom? Elven wisdom – the stuff of legends, and Abren's blood inheritance!

Where was it now?

The waters rose round the square, beaten on by the wind. In it, Abren could have sworn she heard the baying of the Cŵn y Wbir. Sworn she heard the mountain man's voice, calling that she could stop it all by giving herself back to the flood. Right here, right now, jumping the jump that really mattered, and then it would just be between the two of them again and nobody else need get hurt.

Abren took a step, and might have jumped. But suddenly – as if he realised what his long-lost daughter was in danger of doing – the Chadman grabbed her hand. She struggled to break away, but he wouldn't let her go. The wind lashed into him, twice as fiercely as before, but it was as if he had decided to be her father, after all. Decided to be a king, standing up against all comers! No matter that the rain poured down on him in a torrent of new proportions, or that the wind beat hard enough almost to sweep him off his feet – the Chadman clutched Abren with one hand and raised the other to the sky.

He held it up the way he did when feeding the birds. *And down they came.*

Down through the stormy night, as if they owed the Chadman one for all those feasts back through the years! Down from trees and flooded gardens, from gutters and ruined palace walls. Not just black crows in funeral dress, but soft, grey pigeons and pink-and-gold finches, small, brown wrens and red-breasted robins, bright little wagtails and bully-beef magpies, tawny thrushes and spangled starlings. Every colour imaginable, and every shape, birds that sang and birds that were silent, green birds, blue birds, yellow ones, turquoise, brown birds and white.

Yes, even snowy swans, wheeling through the sky as if they had it in them to do more than just kill! And ghostly herons, too, as grey as morning light, and shags like prehistoric creatures, and darting little gold-and-turquoise kingfishers. From the shyest to the boldest – *they all came down.*

And everybody watched them, standing at their windows, holding back their curtains. All the people of Pengwern, watching as a great company of birds, big enough to fill the sky, fell down upon Abren and the Chadman, plucking their clothes, latching on to their hair, stretching their talons across them and getting them in their webby, spidery, clawlike grip.

They watched them get hold of arms and shoulders, neck and hands, legs and knees, and lift them upwards, dragging them off their feet.

Then the whole great cloud – beating like a single pair of wings – rose into the sky. A single bird of power, it carried them through the storm, and nothing could stop them. The Chadman cried as if he'd always dreamt of flying free at long last, but never believed that it would happen. *And certainly not like this!*

And Abren cried as well. Behind her, she could see an astonished Bentley climbing into a tree, the better to watch their journey across town. He waved them on their way, and everybody else waved too – the people of Pengwern, wishing them godspeed.

Abren waved back. The birds carried her over Dogpole Alley, up Pride Hill, past the old town cross, down past the castle and finally to the railway station. Here the flood had changed the landscape beyond recognition. Abren stopped waving, and her heart sank. She had come too late! The main building lay under water, and so did the platforms. The Guinness hoardings stood half submerged, and every trace of the once-great iron railway bridge had gone.

It had completely disappeared.

They flew over the spot where it had been. Abren looked down, imagining thick, black waters flowing between the bridge's hidden arches and its girders, filling its chasms and soaking through its dark places. She imagined it finding all the hidden corners and filling them with black poison, clogging up the stairways and flooding the waiting rooms fit to burst.

Nobody could survive those flooding waters. *Not*

even Old Sabrina could hold them back.

The birds circled the abandoned waiting rooms, and Abren could have wept. One half of the roof remained, but the other half had caved in. There was no sign of Old Sabrina, but as if the birds didn't realise that the battle was over, they deposited Abren and the Chadman on the remains of the ridge, between the chimney pots. Then, as if their job were done, they rose back into the sky – not a single tight cloud any more, but every bird for miles around making its own way home.

The Chadman waved a wild goodbye, as if he hadn't realised yet what Abren could see plainly – *that they had come too late.*

'I always dreamt of heights,' he said. 'Of tightrope walking between spires. Of flying over rooftops. But I never thought I'd do it!'

'You always were a dreamer – *and a fool!*' a new voice said.

They turned around – and there was Old Sabrina! She sat propped like a broken doll against the chimney pots, her feet stuck out beneath her skirt like bits of perished rubber, her clothes tattered and soaked, her eyes as flat as stitched-on buttons, and her head twisted at a funny angle as she looked out over the flood.

The Chadman saw her – and the smile froze on his face.

'Well may you look like that!' she burst out. 'You cruel deceiver, you – thick with lies and syrup-promises! Look what you have done! All these years far from my mountain! And all these years without my child! Never laughing, always grieving. Never

231

dreaming that I might find her. And now I have, *and it's too late!'*

Old Sabrina glared at the Chadman from underneath her mop of bird's-nest hair. She could have killed him with a look. And, glaring back, he could have killed her too.

'Look what *you've* done to *me!* All those years trapped in those ruins, knowing I could never get away. Never have the chance to make a fresh start. And growing older by the day and week and year! And when I do escape at last – *here you are!* Witch! Bitch! Daughter of Plynlimon – I knew from the first day that I'd never get away from you!'

The Chadman shook – a bag of bones rattling with rage. Old Sabrina turned her bitter face away.

'Tell your father that I won't forgive him,' she said, addressing Abren. 'Tell him it's too much to ask. I *won't* forgive what I can't forget. And I *can't* forgive what I won't forget!'

It was like a trap, and Old Sabrina caught in it.

'Tell Effrildis that I don't want forgiveness!' the Chadman said, addressing Abren too. 'Not now, after all these years. I would have given anything for it once, but it's too late. *All I want is to be left alone!'*

Abren's mother snorted. *'Tell your father* that there *is* no Effrildis! Not any more. Tell him that she's gone, and now there's only Old Sabrina!'

As she spoke, the wind blew into her, tugging the hair back from her face so that what she had become was plain to see. The Chadman looked into her face, bleached white with pain and age and misery. He flinched, and stepped back.

'Tell your mother that I'm not responsible for this. I

never meant to harm her. If I deceived her, I only did it for love!'

Old Sabrina drew in her breath. 'Love!' she hissed. *'You did it for love? Why, tell your father that TRUE LOVE NEVER LIES!'*

For a moment, Abren thought that the old woman would hurl herself across the roof and start a fight. But then the storm did it for her. It came sweeping along the roof to send them crashing into each other like weapons of war. They would have destroyed each other, sliding down the roof, locked in battle, if Abren hadn't realised what was about to happen. She got between them, grabbing her mother on one side of her and her father on the other – and clung on to them for dear life.

And they clung on to her too – desperately holding their daughter as the wind tried to drive her off the roof. And she was safe between them because they'd never, ever, let her go. Not again. And suddenly, despite themselves, despite their crazy, mixed-up feelings and the past that lay behind them and the things they couldn't forgive – *they were a family!*

They were Abren's family! Maybe not the one she'd hoped for, but hers all the same. She held them as if nothing could ever prise them apart – not the flood beneath them, nor the mountain man, nor the legend built around their lives calling for a tragic ending. Not even Gwendolina's curse could prise them apart, for they were breaking it right now, locked together in something far deeper than an embrace.

Abren knew what they had done as soon as the wind dropped. She looked up. The rain was drying in the sky and the clouds were rolling away like BC boys who'd been stood up to. Beneath her, the waves began to still, and the swollen flood waters calmed into a vast silver sea.

Abren cried out in astonishment. All around her – from towers to rooftops and attic windows – the people of Pengwern cried out too. And Abren knew that she would never forget them. Never forget this moment, which they shared together.

She turned to share it with her parents too – with Effrildis and the king of Pengwern. But the roof was empty. She stood alone. Her mother had gone, and so had her father. The past had passed on, leaving nothing but a handful of dust settling on the chimney pots like debris from a storm.

Abren took it up, rubbing it between her fingers. Just a pinch of dust, but she felt it full of life and stories, memories and peace at last. It was all that she had left of the past. *But it was enough.*

The upriver trow

The morning stars melted and the sunrise edged over the rim of the sky. The swollen river shone like a sapphire in the first pale light, and Abren sat high above it, between the chimney pots. She would never know where the river ended, twisting out of sight. Her journey was over. She didn't belong here in this new day. She had done what she was meant to do. There were no curses to keep her here any longer.

Abren rubbed the feathered edge of her blanket against her cheek, looking at its embroidery. Had Effrildis realised, she wondered, that when she'd stitched her daughter's blanket she had charted out her life? Here it all was, the mountains and rivers, the birds and trees – even the town of Pengwern, rising like an island in the river's horseshoe loop.

And now it all was over. Abren waited to turn to dust, just like her mother had done, and her father, the king of Pengwern. They hadn't lived to see the sun come up over their town. But here it suddenly was – and the whole town was cheering as if seizing the perfect moment for a celebration. Maybe not with fireworks in the Quarry Park, toasting the sun with tea and coffee rather than champagne. But a better celebration than any stroke of midnight could ever be! For they were toasting new life, and the passing into legend of a moment which schoolchildren would write poems about one day.

But none of them would know what had *really* happened here in Pengwern, any more than the TV cameras knew, circling overhead, thinking that they'd seen it all. For what they knew was all they'd seen – a cloud of birds doing something odd on a day when nature was freakish anyway. They didn't know that what had happened here was a miracle of hope against all odds, and freedom not to hate.

A bell rang out. A solitary bell – and surely rung by Fee! Now would be the moment when Abren turned to dust. She braced herself. This surely was it – the bell of history tolling for her, and the words it tolled were:

'Time for home, don't you think?'

When Abren finally realised that a voice was calling her, she looked down. There sat Sir Henry, bobbing in his coracle.

'Anyone would think you liked it up there among the chimney pots! Come on! Can't you hear me? I said *time for home!'*

He put aside his paddle and held out a pair of long, skinny arms. Abren looked at them, and knew they wouldn't let her go. She looked into Sir Henry's eyes, full of laughter, as ever, and suddenly she knew that not all stories ended at the perfect moment, with the whole town cheering and church bells ringing.

She slid down the roof, crash-landing in the coracle. Sir Henry caught her, set her on the seat beside him, and started paddling through the waters, steering a course for Compass House. They passed submerged pubs and shops, scarcely recognisable by their roofs and chimney pots, passed the castle and the library and the old town cross, reached the old town walls and started along them.

Here the flood waters had retreated, and they could walk along the narrow pavement – Sir Henry with his coracle slung over his back, waddling like a giant turtle, and Abren carrying the paddle. The walls were silent, with not a car about and only the first few people venturing out. They reached Compass House and the tidemark on its wall showed how far the flood had risen. Sir Henry opened the front door, and to Abren's relief, the hall was just as fresh and bright as usual.

The same, however, couldn't be said for the kitchen at the back, which was brown and slimy, and stank. The waters had gone down, but it looked bereft. Everything of value had been dragged upstairs, the curtains had been hoicked up on their poles, the stove was out and the warm, humming room – once the heart of the house – was like a silent ghost.

'Where's Pen? Why's everything so quiet? *Where's Phaze II?*' Abren asked.

'They're in the garden.'

Sir Henry gave Abren a funny look. It was almost as if something terrible had happened and he didn't know how to tell her. She dashed outside. The garden lay under water, right up to the top terrace. There wasn't a soul in sight.

'*Where are they?*' she cried in a panic.

Sir Henry smiled for an answer, and gave her another funny look. He threw his coracle down on to the water and said, 'You'd better get back in.'

Abren did as she was bidden. Her heart was thundering. They paddled out across the garden, and if something terrible *had* happened, Sir Henry was remarkably calm about it. He even paused to show

Abren how to manoeuvre the coracle by herself, holding the paddle straight in front of her and twisting the wooden knob at the top.

It was an effort at first, and the coracle spun like a corkscrew. But then Abren got the knack and they began to move forwards in a gentle dipping motion, drawing level with a cluster of trees which had their roots deep down in the hidden lawn. Suddenly, between the trees and in the place where the boat shed should have been, riding high upon the water – Abren saw a boat.

It wasn't one of Sir Henry's coracles, nor one of the dumpy river cruisers washed up by the flood. It was a sailing boat. An old-fashioned wooden vessel made of painted planks, its flat hold lying in the water, its single mast rising into the morning sky.

Abren shivered at the sight of it. The boat was like another jigsaw piece falling into place. She pulled round her blanket, and there was its perfect match – there, embroidered by her mother, as if to say that her story wasn't over yet!

Abren turned back to the boat, and a figure rose up on the deck. It was Phaze II. He half-smiled at her, and she half-smiled back, thinking that he didn't look like a lost puppy as he had done when she'd last seen him, with all the stuffing knocked out. But neither did he look like what he had once been – a wild boy, creeping through the darkness in a ragged black coat.

'What are you waiting for?' he called. 'Aren't you coming on board?'

Abren didn't need to be asked again! She clambered on board, with Pen to help her up as well as Phaze II. They showed her everything, from foredeck to aft, and from crew cabins to the master's one, with its little window looking into the hold, its cupboard-berths and its little stove.

'Where did you get this boat? Did you make it?' Abren said.

'I didn't make *her*, I repaired *her*. And she's not a *boat*, she's a *trow*,' Sir Henry said. 'An upriver trow, and the very last of them, restored in memory of the days when Sabrina Fludde was the queen of rivers. Half a lifetime's work, I hate to admit – but she's finished at long last! I never thought I'd see the day. And I certainly never thought the river would launch her like this – single-handedly!'

He showed them what the river had done, smashing down the boat shed and sweeping away everything but his precious trow. Abren asked if she had a name. He looked her straight in the eye, and said there could be only one – and that the name which she'd had all along:

'*The Princess of Pengwern.*'

Elvers

They would set off on their maiden voyage after breakfast, Sir Henry said, and prove his armchair critics wrong about sailing on a silty river which wasn't deep enough. Pen returned to the house in the coracle, to fetch them provisions. Sir Henry found a pair of missing side-sheets on the water, and a massive paddle – which he called a sweep – without which, apparently, no river journey could be made in safety.

Before they set out, he gathered his little novice crew around him for a basic lesson in trowmanship. The *Princess of Pengwern* was like a tree, he said. Her *hull* was her root, digging down in the dark, her *mast* the trunk, her *yard* the branches, and her sails – or *sheets* – the leaves shaking in the breeze. Her foredeck stood at the front, or *bow,* and her aft deck at the back, or *stern. Port* was left, and *starboard* right.

Then he showed them how to raise and lower the anchor, loose the ropes which lowered the mast, and steer using the tiller. Talked about wind, and how to turn the square-rigged sail, and about the current, and how the sweeps would help them not to run aground.

He also showed them how to put on life-jackets, and while they were busy tying each other into knots, he released the bowline and poled the *Princess of Pengwern* round so that she could start her journey stern first, trailing the anchor to slow them down until they'd got used to the fast-flowing river. Then he called that the day was getting on and they should leave immediately.

Just as they were departing, however, Bentley appeared. He climbed over the side gate and ran along the terrace, waving his arms and shouting in anguish, 'Don't go without me, Abren! *Not again!*'

He had a point. Abren laughed at him and waved back, pleading with Sir Henry, who gave in at her insistence and fetched Bentley in his coracle. Abren marvelled that he'd known about them setting sail. He laughed back at her.

'Everybody knows!' he said. 'Look up at the town walls. What else has anybody got to do until the flood goes down?'

Abren looked up, and the walls were crammed with silent figures waiting for the moment when the *Princess of Pengwern* would set off. At the sight of them all, Sir Henry grew inches taller. He was the master of a trow! He had a full complement of crew members and every needful provision. And not only that, but the weather promised fair.

They waved goodbye to Pengwern, and Sir Henry untied the last rope so that the little trow could inch out into the water. Suddenly the figures on the town walls were silent no more. The last trow on a river which had once been full of them! They clapped and cheered and waved. Abren could see even Mena waving, and Fee piped them out, wearing his Paddy McBytheway hat.

Abren smelt adventure up ahead. She looked at all the people honouring the days when the river had been a busy thoroughfare. They'd come to remember the past, but something new was happening, too. *And only she knew.*

Abren shivered. The little trow dipped her mast to pass beneath first the crowded English Bridge, then the dark underbelly of the railway bridge. More quickly than she could ever have imagined, Pengwern lay behind her. The mast arose again, as if the trow were waving goodbye, and Abren felt as if the whole town were waving back – not just the people on the bridges, but the trees and houses, churches and cinemas, schools and pubs and old town walls.

She turned away reluctantly, and suddenly a new world waited for her – one that she'd only ever glimpsed from the girders, and now here it was. The *Princess of Pengwern* moved downriver as if taking possession. And no matter that the waters beyond the town were choppy and full of hidden currents, Abren felt as if she were taking possession too. She dipped between banks on a roller-coaster of a ride, while Sir Henry yelled commands and the trow bobbed and careered in her clumsy novice hands.

She laughed and panicked, slipped and fell, despaired and wept with sheer exhilaration. It was the start of a long and exhausting day. On a straight stretch of the river, she helped turn the yard to face the wind so that the *Princess of Pengwern* could show them what she was capable of. It was a marvellous moment – the square sail full and the trow racing downriver.

They sailed into a gorge with the wind behind them, and out again, across open waters where the swollen waters formed a massive lake, under cliffs and around sand banks which lay unmarked on Sir Henry's charts.

Past boatmen's inns they sailed, where poachers once had sold ill-gotten salmon in the porch; along lonely stretches of river where the only signs of life were wild spring flowers and budding willows; past riverside houses with gardens still under flood-water; past farmland and woodland, hills and roads, villages and towns.

Sometimes the river was easy, and all they had to do was follow it. But sometimes it was wild, and they had to drop the sail, lower the anchor, man the sweeps – and hope for the best!

'You think this is tricky!' Sir Henry yelled. 'But this is nothing compared to what you'll feel when you meet the fickle currents of the Severn Sea!'

Night approached and despite all efforts to the contrary, they were still afloat. Sir Henry brought the *Princess of Pengwern* into a quiet, tree-lined haven where he leapt on to the bank and fastened them at bow and stern. Darkness fell, the moon rose over them and the river carried on its way, silvery and magical.

Bentley sat in the bow, playing the saxophone. Sir Henry smoked a coltsfoot pipe. Phaze II disappeared, off on a walk somewhere, and it fell to Abren to stoke the stove and turn tinned meat, beans and carrots into a one-pot stew. Eventually, Pen came down to the cabin to help her. She was unusually quiet, and an awkwardness hung between them. Abren knew what was the matter, but didn't know how to put it right. She had a story to tell. She owed it to them, and it hung between them like a shadow. Things she'd done, and things she'd found out about herself. But she couldn't find the words to start.

She left the one-pot stew simmering, and went off on a walk too, jumping on to the bank and slipping between the trees. Back upriver she could see a house which they must have passed some time ago. It was the only one in sight and she sauntered towards it, drawn by its small squares of yellow light. The moon shone down on her, and she watched the shapes it cast upon the water, so lost in thought that she didn't see the man until they'd almost walked into each other.

He was coming from the direction of the house, striding through the long grass and humming to himself. But Abren didn't even hear him either, and if it hadn't been for the familiar smell of coltsfoot she mightn't have noticed him until it was too late.

But she caught a whiff and looked up, expecting to find Sir Henry out walking too. And there was the man, right in front of her. A long white stem stuck out of his mouth, and a wisp of smoke curled out of its clay bowl. He smiled without taking the pipe out of his mouth – an old man, as small as a child, wearing a pinstripe suit with a waistcoat, watch and chain.

'Are you with the trow?' he asked. 'Because if you are, I've cooked you these. Cooked them for you special. Caught 'em with my lantern last night. Must've known that you were coming. Though I can't imagine why – there hasn't been a trow past here for years. Not since I was a boy!'

He held out his hands. In them Abren saw a black pot lined with newspaper, inside of which lay a pile of something white and thin – not chips, as she first thought, but something more like strands of spaghetti.

'*What are they?*' she asked cautiously.

'They're elvers,' the little man said. 'Baby eels. Their

home's way off in the Sargasso Sea, but they do their growing-up here in the river. Unless the fisherman gets them first, of course! Like I did last night. *Here you are.*'

He thrust his gift at Abren, who found herself clutching not a pot, after all, but a bowler hat turned upside-down!

'They're a real tasty treat,' the little man said.

'I'm sure they are,' Abren replied, trying not to shiver at the thought of eating baby eels whose struggle to grow up had ended in an old man's hat. 'You must come and share them with us.'

The little man didn't say no. Perhaps he'd caught a whiff of coltsfoot coming from the trow. He followed Abren back to it, and he and Sir Henry greeted each other like long-lost brothers – fellow claypipe men sharing the secret pleasures of a good smoke.

The elvers were delicious, too – far better than the one-pot stew. Everybody ate them, even Abren, for all her qualms. Maybe it was the fresh air that did it, or the fact that she hadn't eaten much over the last few days, but she was starving hungry. After she'd finished all the leftovers, the little man removed the newspaper from inside his bowler hat, wiped it clean and gave it to Sir Henry. It had been his father's hat, he said. All the old trow masters wore them. It had been the badge of their trade.

Sir Henry took the bowler hat as if it were made of gold. He put it on his head at the little man's insistence, and for all his claiming that he wasn't worthy, he wouldn't take it off again. It was getting late by now, but with his new hat on his head and his pipe in his mouth he plainly didn't want to go to bed.

Neither did the rest of them. It was getting cold as well as late, but none of them wanted to shut themselves away, fore and aft, in their cabins. Pen invited the little man to tell them about his boyhood days when trows still sailed the river. The little man started talking, and the river rocked them. Abren found herself drifting into a strange, contented half-sleep – only to come to herself again with everybody looking at her.

'What is it?' she said.

'Our friend here's wondering about the flood. He's never seen the likes of it in all his days. *I said that you could tell him all about it.*'

It was Phaze II who spoke for all of them. Phaze II giving Abren the chance to explain herself at last! Abren looked round at them – Pen curled against Sir Henry, Bentley absent-mindedly nursing his saxophone, Phaze II staring at her as if he'd known all along that she had a story to tell, but he'd never asked. Never pushed it. *Not until now.*

And now was the right time! Abren could tell. She ran her finger down the frayed edge of her comfort blanket. Even the little man was watching her as if there were things that he, a stranger, wanted to know. This was her chance to tell them all about herself. To tell it all.

And so she did.

Under angels' wings

In the early hours the little man went home, disappearing into the darkness as he had come, humming his tune and puffing on his pipe. When they awoke next day, his house stood quiet against the river bank without a sign of life.

It was a windless morning and they cast off at first light, with a long day ahead of them according to Sir Henry. The river was still high, and as smooth as glass, and they flowed silently down it with a sense of wonder. It was as if Abren's story had touched them all. Bentley played his saxophone, and Abren sat in the bow looking straight ahead. She'd thought that she might turn to dust when she'd told them everything she had to say – but here she still was.

Bentley gave up playing and came and sat beside her, not a word between them but for just this one day she was his 'cousin from away, come to stay'. That night they moored under Wainlode Cliff. It would be just as long a day tomorrow, sailing into the estuary, so they bunked down early. The sky was clear, the moon as full as a moon could be and the river swelling under the trow. They had reached the tidal passage of the river, and Abren could feel it turning under her as she fell asleep.

Next morning she was woken by a sprightly breeze which knocked the ropes and shook the leaves in the trees. The *Princess of Pengwern* bobbed on the river, as if impatient to get away. Everything felt different. They left the tall pink rocks of Wainlode, drawn by the current and driven by the breeze. On one side of the river a row of willow sticks had been pushed in to mark the edge of a sandbank. They steered around it, travelling out into deep waters where the cross-currents were tricky and all hands were required to work the sail and man the sweeps.

Later, standing at the tiller with Sir Henry, Abren asked about the sea. She had been looking for a first glimpse of it around every bend in the river, but hadn't even caught a whiff of salt. Sir Henry said that it wasn't far now – but first they had to get through Gloucester.

Abren hadn't known that Gloucester existed, let alone lay ahead between her and the sea. But no sooner had Sir Henry told her about its significance in the river's history than she saw it up ahead, and felt it drawing them out of the river's quiet havens into public view. Chimneys, spires and roofs appeared, roads and pavements and towing paths where curious passers-by stopped to stare. Abren saw offices and factories, apartment blocks and houses, caught a glimpse of warehouses, saw a busy road bridge up ahead and a lock beyond it, with massive wooden gates. Here a crowd stood watching the *Princess of Pengwern* making her way downriver.

Abren couldn't wait to carry on past the lock, saying goodbye to Gloucester as quickly as possible. But Sir Henry shouted for the sail to come down, the anchor to be dragged, and the *Princess of Pengwern* poled round so that he could steer her out of the fast-flowing centre of the river, towards the lock gates. A bell rang in the lock-keeper's cabin, and the traffic stopped to let the road bridge rise and let them through.

'What's going on? Why aren't we carrying on down-river? Where are we going?' Abren asked.

Sir Henry didn't answer. His bowler hat in place, he steered the *Princess of Pengwern* into the arms of the lock. Its massive wooden gates, built to withstand tons of water, crashed shut behind them, cutting them adrift from their journey. Abren felt as if the lock's concrete walls, stretching high above her, were a prison cell – and the lock-keeper her gaoler.

'*What are we doing?*' she cried out.

Nobody heard her. They were too busy watching the water level rising and the *Princess of Pengwern* moving up and up until they could suddenly see where they were going – into a dock with pleasure cruisers berthed in rows, and warehouses converted into shops. The water in the lock filled up to the top, and the *Princess of Pengwern* prepared to inch out into the dock. A little tug came and helped her, leading her across the harbour basin to berth beside a tall sea schooner. Washing hung from the schooner's rigging, and the tang of the sea wafting off it was unmistakable.

The sea at long last! Abren strained to catch a glimpse of it down the dock, as if its breaking waves lay somewhere just beyond the schooner.

'We'll stop for lunch,' Sir Henry told them all. 'Stock up on provisions and stretch our legs. Then meet back here at two o'clock, and make our way down the canal. If we're lucky, we'll get a sunset sail on the Severn Sea. But if not, we'll moor the night at Sharpness ready for the morning.'

The others were excited – but Abren only heard the one word.

'*Canal?*' she gasped. 'But what about the river?'

'The river's treacherous between here and the sea,' explained Sir Henry. 'Full of rip tides and quicksands. Only the most experienced master mariners would have sailed down it in the old days, even when the trows were manned by crews who knew the river like the back of their hands. And that excludes us, I think we'd all agree!'

He looked round at them, everybody grinning as if they did, indeed, agree. *We've done the best we can*, the general opinion seemed to be. *And it's been a wonderful experience! And we'd like to make it to the sea, so let's go by canal. Given what you say about the river, it makes good sense.*

It might have made good sense to everybody else, but not to Abren! She turned away. To her it seemed like *giving up*. Bentley spoke for the rest of them, thanking Sir Henry for their great adventure. But he didn't speak for Abren.

She disembarked at the first opportunity, making off down the wharf as soon as their backs were turned. She didn't know where she was going, and didn't really care. What she wanted was time alone, to think. She wandered past old customs buildings, corn merchants and flour mills which now were turned into restaurants, hotels and shops. At the end of the first dock she found a second one, and between the two of them she came across a church with a bell hanging over it and an open door.

'The Mariners' Church,' said the notice nailed to the door, 'welcomes travellers.'

Abren slipped inside, wondering what sort of welcome she could expect. Inside she found a simple, bright room which was cosy but worn, its smell of polished wood reminding her of the cabins on the *Princess of Pengwern*. She sat down on a pew with a bursting cushion, and lost herself in questions about her journey and why it had suddenly gone all wrong.

Over her hung a tapestry commemorating centuries of men, women and children who had lived and worked upon deep waters. Abren stared idly at its woven sunshine and gulls, boats and fish, flowers and stars, sunrise and sunset. They reminded her of her little comfort blanket, and she absent-mindedly fingered its frayed edge. At the bottom of the tapestry was a row of figures woven in every imaginable size, shape, costume and colour, all holding hands and dancing over waves which looked like wild white horses.

Abren looked at them, and remembered the picture in the library book – the one of the girl who had reminded her of herself. Now she saw herself again in these dancing figures. Saw the child who'd arrived in Pengwern not knowing who she was. The one who'd lived with Bentley and been his cousin from away. The one who'd hidden in the limbo-land beneath the railway bridge. Who'd found out all about her past by reading a poem picked up off the floor.

She saw the child who always blamed herself, even when things weren't her fault. And she saw the child who'd made it through. Made it without cutlasses and amber tea and mountain bees. Made it despite everything.

Abren left the church, knowing that her journey hadn't gone wrong. She'd reached its end, that was all. The end of the story, with all the jigsaw pieces put together, *and the start of a new one*. Without a backward glance, she hurried between the docks, knowing exactly what she was going to do.

Back at the *Princess of Pengwern*, nobody was about. Abren took off her little blanket and left it with a note, saying that where she was going she no longer needed charts. Then she untied the coracle from the stern of the trow, hauled it over her back in just the way Sir Henry had done on the town walls, and waddled off like a turtle.

At the end of the wharf, she slipped through a passage between the lock and the main road, found a footbridge beyond it and slid down to the river. Here she dropped the coracle into the water, holding on to the towing rope and prepared to jump in, steadied by the paddle.

'*Where d'you think you're off to this time, then?*' a voice said.

Abren looked up the bank, and there was Phaze II. He stood with his arms folded over his chest, his expression suggesting that Bentley might forgive her for walking out on him last Christmas – and now doing it again – *but he had had enough!*

'It's not that I want to walk out on you,' Abren said, blushing at being caught. 'It's just that I've got to go. There's a new adventure waiting for me up ahead!'

'Perhaps you're not the only one who's waiting for a new adventure,' Phaze II said.

'Perhaps I'm not. But this one's mine. I've got to make it on my own. And it's going to be dangerous! You heard Sir Henry,' Abren said.

'You heard him too!'

'I know I did. *But I've still got to go.*'

Phaze II glared at Abren. She thought of all the things she didn't know about him, starting with his real name, and ending here with his wanting to come too.

'You can't just leave me. You don't understand. Our stories belong together,' he said.

'I'd let you come if I only could. Believe me, I would.'

Abren jumped into the coracle. Feeling guilty and wretched, she pushed it out from the bank and left Phaze II behind. He stood and watched as she clutched the paddle, trying to remember what Sir Henry had taught her. She turned her eyes away from him and fixed them straight ahead. If she looked back, she would go back. And then she'd never make this all-important journey which was hers alone. Never dance the dance or find the new adventure.

Abren paddled on determinedly. The tide was at its highest, on the turn and ready to help her on her way. It got hold of the little coracle and whisked it down-river with no chance of turning back and very little need for paddling skills. Abren smelt the sea again – not a distant whiff, but full and strong and waiting for her up ahead.

She lifted her head and smiled a smile like Pen's – there for all the world to read and impossible to shift! The world viewed from the river was a wondrous place, full of life and colour, ever changing, ever bright. She saw a reedy sandbank where herons dipped, and a spring-green woodland where walkers threw sticks to their dogs. Saw meadows full of cattle and swaying wild flowers, and the sky stretched over everything like an enamelled jewel.

Only when Abren reached a graveyard of old trows did a shadow fall over the journey. At first she couldn't make out what those shapes were, half-rotting among the brambles, disfiguring the bank. But then she saw the stark remains of a massive hull, and realised that this was what the *Princess of Pengwern* must have been like before Sir Henry rescued her.

The coracle carried her away from it – but the shadow remained. Abren passed a lonely flatland without a soul in sight. Saw a train against a bare cliff. Saw a church without a village, and a power station built upon an empty shore, on the edge of a silent lagoon where nothing stirred and nothing grew.

The river was widening all the time, twisting and growing, and the shores were disappearing like distant lands. Abren drifted on, feeling strangely gloomy and unsettled, despite the smile still stuck across her face. The afternoon was closing in, the sun was lowering in the sky and the coracle felt heavy and tired. For some reason, it seemed to drag rather than dash. The sea felt close – but the coracle seemed to hang back.

Abren gripped the paddle doggedly and twisted it through the water. A lock came into view – a great black thing protruding into the river and blocking her view. She imagined Sir Henry's canal beyond it, and looked in hope for the mast of the *Princess of Pengwern*. But for all that she longed to see her friends again, she found the lock empty as she drew level with it.

She carried on, strangely disappointed for a girl who'd wanted to make this journey on her own. The tidal current took her round the end of the lock – and she found herself facing the Severn Sea. The land fell away and the estuary opened out, as pale and silky as a huge pearl. In the distance Abren could see a bridge stretched over it. The last bridge on the river – and soon she would have left it behind! Abren looked at its copper cables, shining mint green in the evening sun.

The bridge seemed to stretch for ever, with no visible starting point or destination.

Suddenly she began to cry. Maybe there were cars upon that bridge, travelling on for ever, and people too. But it looked so empty from down here on the river. Not a soul in sight not even another boat. Abren drifted towards the bridge and the white-topped waves all around her ran lonely lives against the setting sun.

Abren rocked and bobbed and drifted on, feeling lonely too. The bridge drew close. Beyond it was the Severn Sea, and behind her was the river. She had nearly made it, at last! Nearly done what she'd set out to do! She turned to take a final look back upriver towards Plynlimon.

Here I am, she thought, as if the mountain man could see her even here. *I made the journey, and you didn't stop me!*

It should have been her final triumph, but the moment just felt empty, with no one to share it. In the distance, Abren could have sworn she heard the mountain man having the last laugh, as if he could have told her that even if she won there'd be a price to pay. A price for everything!

Abren raised her fist at him, clenched as if to say that no matter what – alone or not – he could never keep her down. And, suddenly, as if the last laugh were hers after all, she saw something in the water. It bobbed behind the coracle, travelling in its wake, caught up in its long towing rope.

It couldn't be – and yet, unbelievably, it was ...

Phaze II.

How he had done it – jumped in after Abren and survived a towing-rope ride along this wild stretch of river – Abren would never know. And neither, in the long years yet to come, would Phaze II ever be able to explain it. But that was what he'd done.

Abren let out a cry. She hauled him in, just about avoiding capsizing the coracle in her hurry to get him on board, punch the life back into him and wrap him in a great wet bear-hug.

Phaze II. *Her friend.* What, how, why ...?

'Yours isn't the only river flowing out of Plynlimon,' Phaze II said. 'And it isn't the only river in this estuary. There are other rivers too, and other stories to be told. *And mine is one of them.*'

It was his final word – at least for now. He settled back in the coracle, plainly exhausted but thoroughly pleased with himself. Abren sat beside him, and the last bridge loomed far over their heads. They had reached it without noticing. Its veil of copper cables shimmered in the fading light, and the coracle slipped under them as if under soft, green angels' wings.

This was the moment when the river ended and the sea began. The moment which Abren had waited for. She threw away her paddle and took Phaze II's hands. Moved out into the sea, and its waves leapt under her like wild white horses. The air was clear and heady, like vintage sea wine, and Abren could hear 'her' tune again. *Hear it playing for the dance.*

She sang along with it, word for word. Tapped her toes and beat time. The sun went down and the moon rose in the sky. The waves began to race, and she felt the pull of a new horizon drawing her across the sea. A new adventure steering her beneath the stars.

Phaze II glanced at her as if to say that he could feel it too.